Garza

Thanks for your fast service!

Happy Reading

To Mark

George

Thanks for

your

service &

Happy Easter

Joe

Diaries of a Soldier

Nightmares From Within

Thomas R. Schombert

Bloomington, IN

Milton Keynes, UK

AuthorHouse™
1663 Liberty Drive, Suite 200
Bloomington, IN 47403
www.authorhouse.com
Phone: 1-800-839-8640

AuthorHouse™ UK Ltd.
500 Avebury Boulevard
Central Milton Keynes, MK9 2BE
www.authorhouse.co.uk
Phone: 08001974150

First published by AuthorHouse 4/19/2006

ISBN: 1-4259-3072-7 (sc)

Library of Congress Control Number: 2006903082

Printed in the United States of America
Bloomington, Indiana

This book is printed on acid-free paper.

TABLE OF CONTENTS

DIARIES OF A SOLDIER

By Thomas R. Schombert

Have you ever wondered why things are the way they are in your life? Well, I have as I struggled for years to figure out the riddles. Fighting through life was not the answer, until one day I came to grips with myself and realized that life has its own destiny written into the scriptures for me.

Thinking that life is all ripples set aside just for me to figure out, I gave into wants and desires only to fall into the snares and traps of life. If you think that you had problems, then try on someone else's shoes for a day and see if you can handle the pain of their life.

Diaries of a Soldier is a gripping true story told through the eyes of a soldier as he lived his life before, during, and after the military, while he served his country proudly. This is not just any ordinary story of a person's life. It is a story of how one man came to grips with his demons inside, faced them by learning how to recognize them, and learned from the mistakes of others, as well as his own. This true and factual story tells the graphic details of struggles in his everyday life, and in intimate details of his daily trials and tribulations as he goes through life as a soldier. This professional soldier tells you how he took the worst of any situation and made it work to his advantage, turning everything into a vast array of knowledge that he used to train thousands of soldiers; inspiring them to strive hard in their lives and stay alive in this cruel world.

In combat, he finds a way to show you all how he dealt with his past and present. Through his own psychological teachings, he works through the pain of life from the past and present. His life teachings have brought amends to thousands of other soldiers and civilians like himself, who suffer from similar letdowns throughout life. This soldier has accomplished many things in his life, with little or no rewards at all in return, yet he finds the courage to give even more of himself, showing that he has the strength to get up by himself and stand on his own two feet. By learning to walk again, if only by himself, he shows the strength in self-healing, while still working through the pain of life's calamity.

Having given his all, this soldier has shown what sacrifice is and how he dealt with it all in the simplest of ways. Self-initiative and hard work helped heal him, as well as thousands of his fellow soldiers as he traveled throughout the world. Through self-psychological mind manipulation and proper word placement in ones mind, his missions in life were completed one after the other, and he let no one ever defeat him inside.

Follow the sequence of events through this trilogy of non-fiction novels. *Diaries of a Soldier*, *Bucket Head*, and *Cannibal Boy* are events written to help those understand just one way of thinking. *Diaries of a Soldier* will take you through the pains of life. *Bucket Head* will haunt you with reality, and *Cannibal Boy* will drop you like a hot rock as you hear the rage inside. With the understanding of all three stories, you will be able to stand up on your own two feet from now on, without the help of so-called doctors and red-tape treatments. Why wait to be treated when you can do it on your own?

CHAPTER 1
Childhood Disasters

It is hard to believe that such a smart-aleck seventeen-year-old adolescent, right out of high school, would even think of joining the armed forces. Nevertheless, I had this obsession in my head, as I grew up, about serving my country and fighting in the wars that would free humankind from themselves. I guess I should have watched what I wished for, because that one day came, when I would be a soldier fighting alongside the best of the best; depositing my seed in the fabric of life for the rest of the world to thrive off of, or at least that was what I envisioned in my mind at the time.

No one really knows how things are going to turn out with the rest of your life until it happens, but for the most part, it was proving to be a challenge. Believe me, life was already starting out for me with a bad hand. With the death of my mother, God rest her soul, life became a need for love, given the vast challenges within it. The hardest part about having a mother who died is what you truly remember at the tender age of five.

We lived in Tucson, Arizona, where work was plentiful, and the town was growing at an alarming rate. I remember having Valley Fever, which turned into pneumonia, and a body temperature of 104 degrees, which rapidly progressed to 106 degrees. Dad was sitting at the kitchen table with some of the neighborhood friends, checking on me every now and then to ensure I was still alive. The doctors back then were not as good as today's doctors, and we did not really have the money to keep me in the hospital after Mom had just given birth to Christopher, my younger brother, who was not more than a few months old.

My older sister, Katherine, was playing with her friends outside our little apartment as the events began to take hold. Little did the family know that life's challenges would play their cards on this family this day. The Grim Reaper began to knock on the door of two very unsuspecting people that sad day. I began to get sick to my stomach, so I got up and ran to the bathroom.

Mommy had just gotten out of the shower as I ran to the bathroom to hug the porcelain god. As I approached the bathroom, I remember seeing Mom look at me with great concern in her eyes as she entered her bedroom doorway. After hacking up what little phlegm I had, I found my way to the bedroom where Mom laid sprawled out on the bed, wrapped in a wet towel. I did what any toddler would when they are feeling sick; they run to Mommy. The ironic thing was that she did not want to answer me each time I called her, so I climbed onto the bed and nudged her. In most cases, the child would be thrown to the ground, tickled, and then smothered in kisses. Nevertheless, this was different as I reached out to touch her hand. I remembered the difference between hot and cold from Mom and Dad teaching me, but Mommy was not supposed to be this cold. I got scared inside. A feeling of emptiness came over me, and I ran to get Dad. I tried to get Dad's attention as I was tugging on Dad's half-worn out flannel shirt, and he told me to go back on the couch and lie down.

"Mommy is sick Daddy."

"What do you mean, Mommy is sick? You are the one that is sick. Now go back to the couch and lay down."

"No, really, Daddy, Mommy is sick. She is not moving, and she is cold."

Dad rushed to the bedroom where he called for Mommy, and she never answered. I stood in the doorway of the bedroom door as I watched Daddy pushing on Mommy's chest hard and blowing into her mouth. By this time, the color in Mommy's face, hands, and feet were a pale blue and white. Daddy yelled to get a doctor here. The neighbors franticly phoned "911" as Daddy tried to revive Mommy. Paramedics finally came and whisked my mother out of the apartment on a gurney as I laid on the couch, crying from being scared, but mainly because my head hurt so bad that it felt like it was going to explode; as any toddler does when they are sick.

Tears filled the eyes of my dad as he came back into the apartment, picking me up and holding me tightly as he carried me to the vehicle, so we could all go to the hospital where Mommy was going. Arriving at the hospital, Daddy was greeted by emergency room personnel, and I was taken away from my father and ushered into another room, where my sister and brother were waiting. I remember hearing Daddy saying, "No, she can't be dead." Little did I know that this would be the last time I would ever see Mommy. Shortly after Daddy stopped yelling, doctors rushed into the same room where Mom and Dad were, as Daddy collapsed to the cold hospital floor in an apparent stress overload. My sister, Katherine, ran to the door to see what was going on as nurses came into the room we were staying. The nurses tried to keep us from leaving the room to find out what was going on with our parents.

With Daddy in total denial over the death of his bride, the nurses began to see another potential problem moving quickly toward death's door. My sickness had been worsening with all the stress, commotion, and I needed antibiotics to knock out the pneumonia that was brewing inside of me. I collapsed onto the floor of the hospital as the nurses talked to Christopher and Katherine. I recall hearing the yelling of the nurses as my father collapsed onto the cold, hard floor from all the stress. The doctors checked my body temperature and found it to be too high for any human to survive. With Dad lying in on the next gurney over, father and son were looked after as the fate of my mother was in God's hands.

"This is not happening to two today," my father said as he rose up out of his stress-induced state.

The doctors worked franticly to keep me alive by introducing drugs and antibiotics into my body. The nurses and doctors then rushed me into another room and submerged me in an ice bath in an attempt to drop my core temperature to normal levels. The doctors continued to work on my father as he was being held back at the door of an isolation room within the ER as his four-year-old screamed his head off from the ice burning its way into his bones.

Passing out from the frigid cold, I awoke to the sound of footsteps and a semi-light stairwell. A man was carrying me down a set of stairs to the basement of what appeared to be the hospital. Reaching the bottom of the stairwell, we approached a huge, plate-glass window with curtains. The man took me off his shoulder, onto which I had been flung and looked at me with tears in his eyes. It was Daddy, crying and praying for me not to die. Daddy pounded on the thick glass window and no one answered, so we proceeded back up the steps from where we came down. Not understanding it then, but looking back on it now, could this be the realm between heaven and hell? Had I passed onto the other side with Mommy, even for a moment? Just as Dad placed his foot on the first step to go back up the steps to the next floor, I saw a woman standing in the very place where Daddy and I had been just a few seconds ago, in a long white dress with long dark brown hair. I called out to the figure that I knew in my heart was Mommy, with the same likeness in every way. Daddy turned quickly to see the image but could not. As we continued up the stairwell to the top, Daddy struggled his way up the winding stairs, carrying me over his shoulder. I could tell my father was drained from the death of his bride and possibly losing his oldest son to Valley Fever and pneumonia. Daddy cried as he carried me from one floor to the other, getting the runaround from the staff in the St. Joseph's hospital.

Reaching the top floor of the pediatrics center, Daddy dropped to the floor in total exhaustion, plunging me to the hard, shiny, cold floor. My Dad's body fell, lifeless, as the stress took over his body. Hospital staff rushed to take me in their arms and to help Daddy to a gurney. An unconscious Daddy and I were ushered into separate rooms, where doctors poked and prodded at me. The panic in their voices set the mood just right, knowing that I was about to die from the high fever. I do not remember much, but I do remember fading in and out of consciousness just before I was submerged in an ice bath again to cool my body from a blistering 105-degree temperature. Death was knocking on my bedroom door as the doctors and nurses fought frantically to save this little boy who had just lost his mother minutes before. The cold from the ice burned through my body, and I struggled to get away from them. Screaming out in pain from the cold that felt like my body was being crystallized. Unbearable discomfort engulfed my entire central nervous system, rendering me unconscious.

I woke up days later, with Daddy sleeping with his head next to my arm, and he looked exhausted. It was not long before the doctors came into the room to check on me. Daddy was awakened to the sounds of nurses and doctors as I laid there wondering what was happening. It seems that my temperature had broken, and I was going to be just fine. Discharge papers were drawn up, and I was allowed to go home from the hospital. Just Daddy and I drove home.

"Where is Mommy? When will she be coming home?"

Much to my surprise, Mommy would not be around anymore. As daddy drove down the road, the tears swelled up in his eyes as he tried to answer me. I took this as the fearful truth and my answer as tears began to filled my eyes as well.

Dear Diary: January 14, 1971
Happy birthday to me. Dear Diary, I am only five, but I needed someone to talk with. I am very sick but not sure how I should feel with all that has happened. Mom just died, "God please rest her soul." I know we have not had much, and we are living day-to-day with what we have, but I just want to say thank you for letting me be alive. At five, some say that you do not remember much; well I am here to say I remember a whole lot more than I am given credit for.

Dear Diary: October, 1972
Dad has been gone an awful lot lately. I think he is thinking of getting remarried. We are planning to move to Avra Valley. He met a woman who is from Mexico, who seems nice and has two kids of her own, a boy and a girl.

Years would pass before a strange-speaking Mexican woman greeted me, and I did not know that this would be my new stepmother, Olga. Dad introduced us all to her, and she seemed okay, for the most part. The only thing a six-year-old kid understands is that this is the parent and now it's time to play.

She had two other children, a daughter the same age as me, and a son who was the same age as my older sister. Becky and Roger seemed cool when meeting them for the first time.

It is strange when you meet someone for the first time, and all their faults seem hidden from you; but in later years, they prove to be nothing but trouble. As a family with a step-family, there is a barrier of concern and trust issues that must be met before you talk, play, or just socialize with one another. This is a typical reaction to any new socialization between humans. This newly found family would prove itself very resilient over the course of its lifetime.

Dear Diary: December, 1975

It's Christmas, and for the first time in years, we are a family again. There were many presents left by Santa under the tree this year. Dad was even home for Christmas this time. Becky and Roger seem a little greedy over what they got. Kathy got her dolls as usual. Chris and I got the cool Tonka trucks that we always wanted and new bikes, you know, the ones with the banana seats and chopper handlebars. Olga seemed happy with Dad, and they ran off to the bedroom to take a nap again. Dad, well he got a lot of gifts from us all. I wish I could give him more, but I am only eight years old and do not have a lot of money. I was hit on the forehead during Little League practice the other day. The knot on my forehead is still hurting. I felt like a total baby face when I was hit, too. I cried so much my dad had to take me home. Nevertheless, it sure did hurt. And the knot on my forehead proved why it hurt, as it stood nearly two inches out of my head like a tumor.

The time that heals old wounds pushes drastic changes to those in dire straights. Dad found a nice trailer in Marana, Arizona, and a small five acres of land to go with it. Here is where we would plant the new seed of our lives. The lingering pain of the past seemed to slip away as we all tended to the family issues at hand on this ranch in the desert. Daily chores were spent feeding the farm animals. Out of all the animals on the ranch, there was only one that I feared the most. Its name was Hatchet; a red-hooded rooster that always pecked at my legs as I walked into the pen, trying to feed it. The ungrateful bastard must have hated me from its birth, because it would chase me around the pen, jumping on my back and pecking me as I ran around trying to get it off me. As small as I was, I just could not run fast enough to get away from this possessed animal. It would squawk all night long, and then crow in the morning, waking everyone up. Nevertheless, everything must come to an end, and this animal's day would soon come. I would cherish the day when it would turn on the hot stake, basting over the barbeque pit, waiting for me to sink my teeth into it. Just my luck, as the hateful creature turned on the stick, its last bite of wizardry turned its hate to my stomach. For about a second, I felt sorry for Hatchet, and then all of a sudden the tables turned on me. This beast of Satan was not about to go down in history as being eaten for dinner. I vomited all over my paper plate as the others watched. The neighbors of the party began to chuckle at me as I rid the mangled pieces from my stomach forever. Once I stopped throwing up, the only thing I wanted to do was go to sleep, but I found my way to the barn where my only true companion stayed. His name was Chief, and he commanded respect from all who stood in his presence. He was a sixteen-hand-high Appaloosa horse that Dad had bought for me a few years back. He never really liked anyone else that rode him, and that might have had something to do with its upbringing. My stepbrother, Roger, always tried to ride Chief, but he was soon bucked off, and Chief would show up at the barn. It was hilarious, if you ask me. Roger was the type that, if you did not give him what he wanted, he took it. Roger grew to be a hateful person within the family, and later in life, that hate would engulf him, confining him to a wheelchair.

Dear Dairy: January, 1976

Diary, Dad did the unthinkable today. He bought me a horse. His name is Chief. From time to time, I would ride him up and down the dirt road to the general store. I am so excited that I have a true friend now. Chris and I sometimes take Chief down the road to our friend's house when we go to play. It is easier than walking, but Roger tried to ride Chief and was bucked off, and Chief came home on his own. Roger came in crying and yelling about how Chief bucked him off. I could not stop laughing at the fact Roger wasn't liked by Chief. I seemed to be the only one that Chief would allow to ride him. Becky was just plain scared of him, so I did not have to worry about her trying to take Chief out for a ride.

We lived in a doublewide trailer in the middle of the Arizona desert. This, in itself, had its challenges, but we managed pretty well, given the odds. Friends were few and far between in the Avra Valley, so we had to make due with what was around us, for the most part. Life's little scary critters passed a good amount of the time, but the one thing missing was other kids to play with. Chris and I grew a huge imagination as we grew up. Spiders and scorpions were one thing, but wrangling a lizard and strapping M-80s to their tail then letting them go back into their holes in the ground; now that was passing the time. Some would say we were completely nuts, but as with anything, it got old fast. Therefore, we worked on other things that took weeks to construct. Tree forts seem to be the ideal hideout from Becky and Roger. From time to time, we had sleepovers, and we would all go up in the tree fort and spend the night under the stars. At least until one of us got scared. That is ironic, given the job that I now hold.

Dear Diary: June 1978

Chris and I finished building our tree fort. It was great, until Becky and Roger came over to tear it all down in one second. It's just like them to destroy all that Chris and I have worked so hard to build. Nevertheless, no worries, mate. Chris and I had other plans in the works already. Not far from the tree fort, Chris, some friends of ours and I, built an underground fortress. We were digging for days. When we had to go in for the night, we made sure to cover up the hole with tree limbs so no one would find it. This fort had it all, except the kitchen sink. We built it just big enough for all five of us to fit, but deep enough to stand up inside. We took timber from the dead trees around the area and some metal fence stakes that held barbed wire up and used them as supports for the roof and laid down tin as the roof over the tree limbs and stakes. We covered that with a thin layer of dirt and put plants back in their rightful place. A tree stump like on Hogan's Heroes *concealed the door. No one was going to find us under the ground, and it was quiet. When Olga became angry, Chris and I would go to the underground fort and stay there all day, eating the candy we had stashed inside the cubbyholes, and drinking Sarsaparilla Root Beer. Sometimes, Olga would call for us and we did not want to go back home, so we stayed in the fort. One time, when Dad was working late, we fell asleep in the hole and forgot to go home. The next day, Olga was really pissed, but she never paid much attention to us anyway, so she quickly forgot about it.*

With Dad gone most of the time on long working trips, Chris and I had nothing better to do than find better and better ways to hide from the evil witch that stood in the doorway, calling our names, knowing damn good and well that we were less then one hundred meters away. When we did not want Becky or Roger to find out where the new tree fort was, Chris and I would spend the day playing out in the dirt with the new Tonka trucks we got for Christmas the year past. G.I. Joe and Barbie were chopped up over a bitter dispute between our older sister, Chris, and I; and neither one of us were in the mood for soap operas.

Dear Diary: July, 1978

I feel sad today. Chris is not here today. He went over to his friend's house. Kathy is gone at her friend's house, too. I have no one to play with. I am alone most of the time, so I just felt like taking the ax in the barn and chopping up Barbie and Ken. I even chopped up my Gumby Doll. I had him too long anyway. I guess I will just go in the house and watch television by myself.

I felt sorry after we chopped up the dolls, because Kathy, my older sister, loved her dolls. They had a sentimental value attached to them, since they came from Dad. He always seemed to get just the right things for us kids every year for Christmas. A few more years would pass, and Kathy turned fifteen. Thinking she owned the world, she just, one day, up and left. I guess she could not take the belt lashings from Olga or the stepchildren's sibling rivalry. Therefore, she took what she could after a huge squabble with Olga and ran from home. Years would pass before anyone would see nor speak to her again. I would virtually be a grown man before she would contact me again. Dad did everything he could to please all of us, trying to keep us all healthy and happy, but sometimes, the future has different plans for all of us. Most of my time after Kathy left was spent sitting in the tire swing, praying for the best and crying my eyes out until Dad got home and I would run up to him, showering him with hugs and kisses. Dad was pretty broken up over his own daughter leaving, given all that had happened in the past, from the death of a bride to the trailer burning down, losing, literally, everything, and having to start all over again, and now, his offspring left home for good. Of course, I could not blame her for leaving. She always felt that everything that Olga's natural kids, Becky and Roger, did was being blamed on her for. Of course, this was the truth, because Olga always had a hand in the spoiling of Becky and Roger, the stepbrother and sister to us, so that Chris, Kathy, and I pretty much stayed to our collective selves. Chris and I spent most of the day with the kids who came from down the long dirt road to nowhere. Our past time was spent building tree fortresses and underground tunnels. This was our hideaway from the wicked witch who once announced herself as the loving stepmother. It was so funny at times when we would hide from Olga, Becky, and Roger, as they called out for us, yelling at the top of her lungs to get our attention; but we rebelled to our hearts content, due to the lack of patience that the witch from the west would have for us if we came running. One minute, we were there, and the next, we would be hidden from the world above. I always loved the part when Roger would get all pissed because he could not find us, and the dumb S.O.B.was literally standing on top of the hidden cave. Then we would hear Olga yelling our names from the doorway a few times over, and we would slowly walk home, knowing she was pissed at us, but also knew she was too tired to whip us after exhausting her efforts on her yelling so hard. Her voice would be half-gone from all the yelling by the time we reach the edge of the barn.

With Kathy now gone, Chris and I would have to take the blunt of Olga's wrath for the three white kids in my father's life. This once-happy home turned to a broken household overnight. As the years went by, the hatred raged in our house as Dad left for work each day. The daily ritual was to stand all of us kids in the kitchen only to force-feed each one of us the most wretched medicine. It was about the same texture as milk, with the taste of oil, and a smell that forced you to hold your nose as you gagged down the elixir of death. All of this torture, to ward off any type of sickness known to man, was quickly chased with a slice of orange and a daily dose of Flintstone vitamins. Boy, did I feel healthy now. "Not in your wildest dreams." How can anything so wretched be good for you?

There were times when Dad was home, and he took Chris and me to the Little League ballgames to watch; unless there was a game that Chris and I had to play. Dad sponsored the team, the Rough Riders, one year. We looked good, but could not play to save the Pope. I remember the time I tried to catch my very first fly ball. The sun was high that day, and I held the glove in front of my face as my Dad said to do.

"Don't be afraid of the ball, son," Dad chimed in, with his two cents.

However, I figured out quickly that you could expect to catch the ball with your forehead by moving your glove at the last second, and hoping the ball went to your glove. After I woke up from being knocked out cold, then crying my eyes out, the coach and my dad wanted me to go back out there and play again with this huge knot on my forehead. We laugh about it now, but boy, was my pride hurt with all the townspeople watching. It didn't take long before I gave up the baseball thing and moved onto jumping trashcans with my bicycle. I had that kind of bike that was ever so cool; the ones with the cool banana seat and sissy bar on the back, and chopper-style handlebars. The front tire, of course, had to be smaller then the rear.

"This was the cool bike, man. I was the hottest kid on the block, all kicked back on my chopper bike, trying hard not to kill my self before Olga got a hold of me. Yeah, right!"

I was hot from the sun maybe, but we had to deal with what we had, and this chopper bike was my ticket to the world. I was going places, man, and that was cool at the time. I remember the time my brother and I were riding together. We were late getting home as we peddled faster and faster. The roads were just freshly graded from the county, and as we approached the driveway, we thought we could get over with just a simple hump in the road. Oh no! Not us. Chris leaned forward as we went over the dirt mound, which raised the tail end of the bike into the air, suspending us as we traveled for about fifteen feet before Chris went over the handlebars, digging his face into the ground. I landed on top of him, and the bike came to rest on top of me, but not until after I was run over by the front wheel and had the right pedal gouge me in the back. After a few minutes of pain and total embarrassment from the crash, we sat there, laughing so damned hard that we almost pissed our pants. If we had flown a few more feet, we would have landed in the cactus that was growing there at the edge of the driveway. In addition, like all good things, we would have to explain to Olga how we got those scratches all over us. Dad would just say, "So, did you learn your lesson out of this?"

Well, as my imagination grew, and my world around me was crashing down, I watched as Olga became more belligerent towards my father. I noticed that Dad would be gone all the time at work, trying to make ends meet for us kids to survive, and Olga nagged him, daily, for more. About the only good thing that came out of that stepmother/stepson relationship was the fact that she made good Mexican food; and she knew how to treat a really bad hangover.

Dear Diary: 1979

Diary, it is a sad time for me now. Kathy has left the house completely. Chris has found new friends to be with all the time, now. I don't want to be around Becky and Roger anymore, because they are just spoiled rotten by their mother, Olga. I have no one anymore. Dad is always gone now. I ask him from time to time if I can just go and hang out with him, but he does not want to take us with him. The fire took all we had and now we have to start over. I do not know if we are going to make it now. Dad seems so sad. He worked so hard to get where we are now. I feel bad for all the animals that were killed in the fire as well. Please

God, make the pain go away. Please help our family to become one again and stop all this hate.

With Dad gone all the time now, the family became more and more distant. I spent more time in front of the television, watching *Gilligan's Island* and *Hogan's Heroes* re-runs, as I spent countless hours playing with the little green toy soldiers that Dad bought me all the time when we went to the general store in town. I could not go riding anymore, because during the house fire Chief died. I mourned for days when I found out that my horse was gone. Memories were lost forever in the fire that shook Avra Valley. In a matter of seven minutes, all that we had was burned to the ground. Nothing was left to salvage, not even the prize 4-H animals that we had raised since they were born. The memories of Mom and Dad together as one would be lost for years to come. Everything, from our clothes to the simple toy, became part of the charred rubble in the center of the twisted, burnt metal that held the main structure of this massive doublewide trailer.

The fire chief rushed to turn off the gas tank that fed the house with natural gas, but it was too late. The heat from the flames was so intense that it was not long before an explosion rang out in the valley, as the gas tank ignited and sent thick, black smoke barreling into the mid-afternoon sky. Dad would never be the same after that night.

The help given from the total community was self-evident, as clothes, money, and food poured in from everywhere. I was thankful for all that we did have, and I prayed for all that we had been blessed with. Dad was hurting deep inside from all that had happened, but the love in Dad's eyes grew as we got older. I could hear it in his voice and see it in his eyes every time he talked to me, and I knew in my heart that he was doing all he could to give us what he could. There were nights when I laid in bed, pretending to be asleep, and eavesdropping on their conversation. I knew it would not be long before Dad would take Chris and me away from there forever. Before Dad would fall asleep, I could hear him praying for us kids and a better life for us all as he cried himself to sleep. I know Dad did all he could to give us what we needed and wanted, and it didn't take long for him to figure out that the three of us were being abused repeatedly by Olga while he was gone all day at work.

Nevertheless, I was not about to have her break me as she did my sister. I stayed to myself outside all day on the weekends and plotted her total destruction with the hundreds of toy soldiers that riddled the living room floor in front of the television set. The abuse was anything, from the simple placing of the blame on the three of us for what her kids did to not feeding us at all, or even worse, to beating us with a fly swatter for no reason as we stepped out of the shower.

Dear Diary: October 1979

Diary, I want to die. I was just raped, and I don't know what to do. It was horrible. The people that did this even live down the road from us. I guess when the things are bad, they can get worse. The trailer burning down, and now this, what should I do? Should I tell Dad, or should I keep it secret. Dad seems to be tired all the time and very stressed out for sure. I am scared, God, and don't know what to do. Help me end all this madness. Make it all go away. I can tell that something is wrong with Dad, and Olga and I hope we move away from here. I don't want to be here anymore.

There were times when I would wish for the raping again that I never told Dad about. I was twelve years old when it happened. Walking home from my best friend's house one day, a stranger who was dating a neighborhood girl chased me from my friend's house, down the dirt trail to my house, and into a secluded area where he could have his way with me.

Screams from my tiny voice fell on deaf ears as this bastard had his way with me. This is a memory that I would carry for the rest of my life. Due to the embarrassment and humiliation, on top of the thought that I might be in trouble for having this happen to me, I held in the pain and knowledge of its happening forever, so that bitter rivalry would forget in time. For years, I thought I had done something wrong and lived with the shame, yet time had its way with me, as well, and taught me differently. I had come to the realization much later in my life that not all that had happened to me was as bad as it really seemed at the time. Everything happens for a reason, and my reason would not be figured out until later in life.

As the relationship with Olga and Dad became more and more bitter, arguments built up within the household. It was no longer the typical money issues or the fact that the other was too tired to do anything. It was more on the lines that each other had allowed themselves to fall out of love and into the passion of other, friendlier people. In this case, I did not blame Dad one bit for finding another. Dad knew inside that the family was falling apart, and he took the necessary steps to make it right when he filed for divorce.

The day of a newly found life reached its pinnacle as Dad pulled us outside to the truck before he went to work. There in the truck was my sister. Dad explained to Kathy, Chris, and I that he wanted us all to pack what we could before he got home from work that day.

"Try to pack after school, and don't let Olga know what you are doing. If she asks, just say you are cleaning up."

That day, Dad returned as Chris and I packed what little we had. To our surprise, Dad was smiling for once in his life. As we ran our stuff out to the truck, we saw Kathy and some young woman sitting in the truck. Dad talked to Olga as we gathered the rest of our belongings and put them in the truck. This was the turning point in our lives, as the five of us drove off into the sunset-lit night without looking back at all. I do not even think Dad looked into the rearview mirror until we hit the city limits of Tucson. The truck ride was quiet most of the way. Dad and our soon-to-be new stepmother Cheryl, seemed to be cool. She was everything that Olga was not. She had looks, and she seemed to like everything about us. She was straight up, one-hundred-percent Italian. Cheryl seemed to give off that feeling that only a real mother could give.

Dear Diary: 1980
Our first night in the new apartment in Tucson with Cheryl, our new stepmother. She seems really cool, and she is really pretty. Oh, and did I mention the really cool Camero she has. Dad and Cheryl look good together. The best part is Kathy came home to live with us all again. Chris and I are playing together more now. We are a family again. I go to a good school in the city now, and I like it a lot. I hope this never stops.

At times, the loss of not having a real mother hurts deep inside but how can you cry for someone you never really knew? It would be years before I would see her gravesite, which I did not even know existed, where I would tell my most intimate secrets to a slab of stone and a brass flower vase. Beside her grave are my grandmother's and grandfather's gravestones. Kathy, Chris, and I grew up moving a lot from place to place, going to various schools, until the day, the three of us would finally graduate high school and move out on our own. With this stepmother, we all seemed to be a family, but with the splitting of a family, the ties grew further and further apart without us even knowing it. There were some good times, but a majority of it was feuding between sister and brother, like the time when my older sister, Kathy, cooked for Chris and I, but I didn't want spaghetti. She was so upset that I didn't want her burnt spaghetti that she threw it in my lap and ran away, thinking she would get away with it.

"Oh, no. Not in this lifetime."

I chased Kathy around the block for almost thirty minutes, but not before I went into the refrigerator and got the eggs that I would beam her with. As I ran, I threw eggs at her, missing every time. With her being bigger than me, I basically ran her into the ground, until she was close enough to pummel her with eggs. Needless to say, she was covered. But don't think I didn't get my share. After she showered and all seemed quiet on the home front, Kathy came out of the kitchen with spoiled tomatoes in an old Tupperware container and dumped it over my head. Chris, who was sitting next to me, played in on it and rubbed it all into my hair and shirt. Therefore, without further ado, I retaliated with an all-out kitchen food fight. Cheerios were everywhere, along with spaghetti and eggs, and tossed salad and dressing. About the only thing we needed then were steaks. But the only thing that would be cooked was us, as Cheryl and Dad walked into the house.

"Busted!"

The dumbfounded look on their faces as Dad and Cheryl walked in the house and saw the total destruction of a home...well, lets us say it was not a funny thing, even though we laughed about it. The disturbing part was that Dad and Cheryl said to clean it up and go to bed after we got cleaned up ourselves. I think they were so shocked that they had to think up a punishment for us all. Oh, it came the next day, in the form of restriction. I thought that we would never get out of the dungeon until we graduated high school. With that said, the good times were over for us all as Kathy moved out on her own and eventually graduated high school away from the household. Chris and I finally settled into one high school, where we shined in sports and academics, and finally graduated. The girls were many for me, and it was no wonder that I would follow the example of my father and have many breakups of my own. I did not see it that way. I aimed to break that chain of agony and defeat that lingered within the family lineage. The saying, "All good things must end," rings true in the hearts and minds of so many. A perfect example of this showed its true colors to me as my Dad and Cheryl began to fight a great deal, and again Dad became unhappy with the fidelity of the pickings he had chosen for himself. Therefore, it did not surprise me when Cheryl and my Dad went their separate ways and decided to divorce. I was starting to think that the girls had it out for my Dad, who in turn was taking their issues out on me when things didn't go their way, but I didn't let that stop me from driving on to the next fish in the vast sea of love. It was not long afterward that I graduated high school and left to join the military.

Cheryl moved on, and I know it hurt Dad, despite that he tried so hard not to show the pain. Dad worked extra hours again to cover up the pain of the past years and the rebound that any rightfully sane person with years of relationship would go through. Anyway, I never understood the reasoning of women, in general, after Dad divorced for the second time, but I was learning from his heartaches. And in turn, I found my own way in life as I made the necessary steps to make a life for myself. I stumbled along the way before my plan became reality, but it was my plan, and I had the ambition to stick to it, despite the torture it was putting me through.

CHAPTER 2
Basic Army

It wasn't long after my high school graduation that the marine recruiters were calling on me to join up. I remembered the days of high school football games, when the marines would march out on the field before the game to display the colors in honor of our brave men and women, as the national anthem played. I never thought I would venture to the side of the marine corps over the army; oh no, not me. I would never change my childhood dream of being a foot soldier in the army like John Wayne and the rest. The blood-sucking vultures got their wish as they finally dragged me into the community building to take my ASVAP test. I scored pretty darn high in all the areas and was given the choice of whatever I wanted to do in the military. There was one drawback to it all: they forgot to tell me that there was a height and weight limit for everything, and that I was too skinny to be in the military. Therefore, despite all the pain of "hurry up and wait" at the community building and MEPS, I was sent packing as a dropped candidate from the military. I had passed everything else with flying colors, but the only thing holding me back was my size. As I stood outside the MEPS building, waiting for the bus to take me home, an army recruiter saw me and asked if I was interested in the army while he lit up a Marlboro Red cigarette. I explained my situation to him, and he was astonished of the scores and by what was happening. I figured that it would make my Dad proud if I would become someone or something. It was not that I had anything to prove to anyone, it was just that I wanted my Dad to see that he had accomplished it all for me, and this was my way of saying thank you. It was my turn to protect him.

The army recruiter shuttled me into the office and sat me down as I fought back the tears of anger. I had failed because of one thing, my size. I couldn't help being so damned skinny, yet that didn't seem to matter to this recruiter. He had a conniving way of doing things, and I could see that in his eyes as he ran in and out of the office, gathering my scores and other paperwork. This would make his day for sure. I was a perfect candidate to add to his quota for the month. All that stood in the way was my size, and that would prove to be an exception to the policy for me in the army. This soldier held my future in the palm of his hand as he waved the mighty pen in my face and asked me what I wanted to do in the army. I wanted to make a difference in my life. I wanted to see the world and be a part of change in the world. In addition, doing this for my Dad was just one of my many reasons to join. In fact, it seemed to be the right thing for me at the time. It helped me become the man I am today, a huge change from that punk kid I used to be. The army as a whole, I give my respect to, but my first choice for joining the military was the Marine Corps. At the time I joined the military, I was sitting in the army office, pondering over whether I should or should not join, but my choices were set for me through destiny. The good sergeant talked to me about the many jobs in the army and what I would like to do. He showed me many videos and books of the hundreds of different jobs that the army had to offer. He didn't want me to feel obligated to join right away if I wasn't ready, so he offered to pay for me to stay one more night in Phoenix and return in the morning to go over some offers.

I took the room and spent the night thinking about how kind this sergeant was to me, and going over in my head the possibilities that were offered and a potential life with the army. I went back to the days of my childhood, when I would play with the green-and-tan toy soldiers in front of the television. On the other hand, there were the times Chris and I would hide from everyone in the tree forts and underground tunnels that we built. As morning crested the mountaintops, the sergeant returned to my hotel door to take me to breakfast. There, in the diner, were hundreds of potential recruits who had made the same decision I did; but these were not just any recruits. These were Army recruits only. It was like an elite club that you had to be in to be there and I was starting to like the feeling a lot. After breakfast, we all gathered in a formation, and actual soldiers marched us to the MEP's station. It was cool seeing it from the inside out, but I was not even in yet. As I waited for the recruiters to call my number, the marine sergeant noticed I was sitting in the army chairs, and he came over, trying to get me to come back to the marines. But I had already made up my mind the night before to give the army a chance. Without skipping a beat, the officers and NCOs of the army-recruiting command quickly ushered me into the office and closed the door behind me. It appeared that this was a cutthroat business to be in; either that, or I was just fresh meat. The nonstop poking and prodding was a never-ending process. The recruiter who found me felt sorry for me and would have done anything to get me in. He said that I had some of the highest scores that he had ever seen in a long time. It made me feel good with the present company I was dealing with. Just to get me in the service with the little frame that I had, I was stuffing rolls of quarters in my pockets to weigh enough to meet the requirements to come into the military. I weighed in at a whopping ninety-eight pounds total, and this was before I took the morning dump. Hey, every bit counts in this line of work.

Dear Diary: September 1986

Hello, Diary. I know it has been some time since my last entry. I have good news. I will tell you all about what has been going on in my life. Well, after the move to Tucson and the divorce between Olga and Dad, we all came back together as a family and moved around a lot from house-to-house and school to school. We even lived in the Foothills. I hated that school, but it was nice living there among the rich for a change. I even had a really hot girlfriend there. Boy, were her parents loaded with money. Cheryl, Dad's new wife seems really cool. She is a clean-freak, though, but it is for the good of us all. The really good news today is that I have graduated high school, and I was accepted into the United States Army. I am excited and scared at the same time. But I need this. I need the change, and I need to get out on my own. Kathy has since moved on after graduating high school and gotten married to a soldier in the air force. Chris is still in school and has a few years left. Well, I can say that I need to move up and grow up. This child attitude is getting to me, so here I go. Wish me luck. Oh, and thanks for being there all those years for me.

Your pal, Thomas Robert "Root Beer" Schombert.

Hey, remember that? LAUGH. Yeah it was cool back then, but I had to change back to the "old me" as I got older. I hope you understand.

I spent the rest of the day eating C-rations and waiting for the final verdict of whether or not I was accepted into the high society of war and death, and believe me, kids this is a real world of high society. The military has its ups and downs, but if you want to go places, then you have to be a part of the experience and go alone with that which has a hold of you. Being a soldier does come with a price, though, as you will soon see by reading on.

The day of hurry-up-and-wait finally ended as the wooden double doors to my destiny opened at the end of the hallway, and two-well groomed sergeants emerged with clipboards and tidy green shirts and pants, wearing highly shined low quarters, with their decorations displayed proudly on the front of their shirts for the entire world to see. The names of the righteous and worthy were called to the room for formal swearing in. If you were not called, then you still had issues that you needed to deal with, but if you were called, your days of waiting were over, and you were now ushered into the limelight of the highly looked-upon and highly regarded.

The glory of having my family name called rang loud in my ears as the sergeant yelled it out. I waited for the sergeant to call it once more before I quickly jumped to my feet and joined the proud citizens standing in ranks within the room, awaiting the final swearing into the active federal service. It took all I had to keep me from grinning ear to ear as we were all motioned to raise our right hand and swear the oath of allegiance:

"I, John Doe, do solemnly swear (or affirm) that I will support and defend the Constitution of the United States against all enemies, foreign and domestic; that I will bear true faith and allegiance to the same; and that I will obey the orders of the President of the United States and the orders of the officers appointed over me, according to regulations and the Uniform Code of Military Justice. So help me God."

Those words could not have stained my heart and soul more than hearing "I love you" from my very own father. Whatever happened to those that believed in this phrase? Whatever happened to those that cared for the nation as a whole? At this point, I was as proud as a man could be. I was a soldier.

Basic training for me was my time to unleash the hate and anger inside, turning it into something productive for once. I took all that I had inside me and, for once in my life, made the final decision to sign on the dotted line. It seemed funny at the time, how good it felt to make a decision on my own, without someone else making all the decisions for me.

Well, I can tell you this, the slaughterhouse is not as bad as some say it is. Within minutes, I had made a decision to become a part of this elite group of people, and it felt good inside. I signed on the dotted line to be a "91A," which is a combat medical specialist. I had always wanted to help people, and I loved the outdoors, but this was going to be an inside job, working in emergency rooms. For the first time in my life, I had total freedom, and I wanted more.

And believe me, kids, there is more. A whole lot more.

I spent the day going through different stations and doctors, and screening out the bad people who were trying to come in the military. I started to make a great deal of friends, as we all felt the pain of the needles, which we were poked and prodded with. The hardest part was waiting for the results to come back. I sat patiently ; well, almost patiently, in the lobby as names were read aloud to come forward. Those that made it were taken to another room, where they were sworn in and taken to the hotels for further processing. I felt sorry for the ones who really wanted to be a part of this elite group, but could not.

So there I was, standing in a room full of men and woman who believed in the same cause that I believed in. We spent the night in the same hotel that I stayed in the night before, awaiting the bus trip to Fort Jackson, South Carolina. This would be my last night of true freedom, as I had known it, for a long time to come.

The next morning came quickly, with the NCOs pounding on the hotel-room doors. I did not have much as far as bags were concerned, so I gathered what little I did have and ran to the formation in the parking lot. Some followed in the same manner, but those who did not were scolded in front of everyone as they slowly dragged themselves to the formation. I was excited to be getting on with basic training, but something that morning told me that I would wish I did not think that. We ate a quick breakfast, and before we knew it, the busses were outside waiting on us all. This was my last chance to say good-bye to Arizona for a while as I boarded the bus. Moreover, the last thing going threw my mind at the time was calling home to tell Dad that I had made it in the Army for sure. The anxiety built up inside as the busses pulled away and I began my long journey within the military life, leaving behind all that I had remembered.

Hours were spent sleeping, if I could, against a hot, smelly, bus window. God only knows what had been on this window, but it was mine for the day. During the trip, I pondered the thoughts of what I could have done better throughout my life as a child, but that was behind me now. I was not much of a talkative person in high school, even though I was popular. I liked to tell everyone that I was not, but the cold, hard, facts were that I dated a few girls who were hot and played sports like any normal kid would. Girls were my game, though. I had this dream that I would marry some day, and then it quickly went away. It was just not for me right now. Anyway, the cold, hard, fact was that I was picked on a lot in school, and the chicks played off that. I guess that was how I became so popular. I never made Prom King, but I did graduate.

Throughout my younger years, I spent a lot of time moving from town to town and school to school. I went to rich school and lived in the Foothills of Tucson, Arizona, which was supposed to be the rich part of the town, to the lower end of town, where we struggled just to keep food on the table. One of the biggest mistakes I could have made in my life was when I inherited a large amount of money, which I pissed away rather quickly on my so-called girlfriend, at the time. I thought I really cared for her, so I did the unthinkable, I spoiled her. With the regret gone now, I turn to the accomplishments that I had now. What I had was due to hard work, sacrifice, and sweat.

After hours of sitting on a cramped bus, we arrived at Fort Jackson, tired and irritable. My first taste of the military would come as the drill instructors jumped on the buses and began barking orders. I remember a few things, but the one thing that really sticks out in my head is the part when he said that I had three seconds to get my shit and get off this bus, "And two seconds are already gone." As skinny as I was, I was not going to piss this guy off any time soon. Gathering what little I did have, I exited the bus and was motioned to the formation in the courtyard. This was where we were all broken down and separated by gender, of course, and service number. The barking never really stopped for me. It felt like it was a new thing for me, even though I had the abuse every day of the week at home from my stepmother, Olga. For once in my life, I was scared, so I did the best thing that any scared person would do. I picked out one of the instructors in the "Smokey-the-Bear" hat and then picturing that person as Winnie the Pooh. I could not help but laugh aloud as names were called. One person I picked out was a five-foot-two, African American male who literally sounded like a Smurf. What was even funnier was that he had a sidekick, an African American female who towered over him. Now here was a female who looked like she could really do some damage. Let us just say that the best part about her was her smile. The six-foot-two female, better known as Drill Sergeant Horn, was built like one of those athletic aerobic instructors that you see on television all the time; you know, the ones that producers use in the fat body commercials. Well, nevertheless, she could smoke the living daylights out of you, and you would not even know it. Moreover, this is what happened daily to me. By the time I graduated basic training, I would be very much in shape. As I tried hard not to laugh at the "dynamic duo," the drill sergeant came over to me and yelled at me so loud that I thought my ears would pop.

"What the hell is so funny, private?"

"Ha, ha, ha, ah...Nothing drill sergeant."

"Well something must be really funny if you are laughing."

I slipped every now and then with a laugh as the brim of his drill sergeant hat tapped my forehead. He was so damned close, I thought he wanted to kiss me.

"I..I.. he, he, ha, don't think you would think it was funny, drill sergeant," I said as I laughed, and small amounts of spit splattered onto his face. You could see the veins in his neck swell as he became more enraged.

"Well then, try me, private. Maybe I want to hear what you think is so funny".

"Waa…Well drill sergeant; I was feeling a little down, so I just pictured you as Winnie the Pooh who talked like a Smurf."

It was then that I knew I would regret that for the rest of my time in the military. The entire formation broke out laughing and could not stop. I even had the other drill instructors laughing, except one; my senior drill instructor, who stood in front of me. I do not remember much the rest of that day after I was hit in the gut and then knocked out cold with just one punch. However funny it was at the time, the others never let me forget it, but at the time, it was the funniest damned thing I had ever said in my life.

Dear Diary: October 1986

Oh my god, what did I just get myself into? I think I just fell into a Satan-worshiping spell that sent me to the first lesson in total mind torture and body damaging. My first day was not so good. Everyone here yells and that is not the worst part. They make you eat more than one person can eat in a sitting. I had to finish within a certain time limit and then shower, shave, and shine boots all within another time limit. If I didn't then I was given physical conditioning in the form of ass chewing and pushups. My arms are hurting so bad right now, if I keep this up for the nine weeks, I think I will be bigger than Mr. World. Good God, man, these people are even crazier then I am. I saw a person tonight get all of his stuff thrown from the top floor, out the window, to the dirt out in the back of the barracks. It had something to do with him living like a pig, and the drill sergeant did not want the rest of us to live like that. Therefore, he slept out in a tent that night. I had better get to sleep before I am caught writing you.

Weeks went by, and I learned a great deal by working with all types of diversities and backgrounds. It was not easy for me, at first, to take orders from another person who had just made the same mistake I had, but in the long run, each one of us became judgmental in our own right. I had already accomplished what I needed to, and it was their turn to prove themselves. It was all up to them, and no one else. That was seemingly selfish, but it was part of life and the learning process. In this business, baby, you have to learn through mistakes. That way you do not make them later when you are needed the most. My own selfish ego pampered me as I thought I was better then the rest. The more I accomplished, the better I became, and I started to think I would be the next ruler of the barracks. It was not right, but at least I could think it and keep it to myself. This is where I gained most of the common sense that was never issued to me. Speaking for some of the others, I cannot say they were issued any common sense at all. Common sense, respect, and other admirable traits needed in life now became second nature. How hard could this job be? Being told where to be and what to do is easy if you think about it. You are woken up, put to bed, told when to eat, exercise, go to the bathroom, shower, and after each day, you are paid for it. What could be better then that?

Some days were tough, but for the most part, all you had to do was listen and learn. I will not say that everything was peachy all the time, but I did learn to go with the flow of things. Having a trained killer literally two inches from your face yelling at you as his drill hat hit you in the forehead was not my idea of a good day, but you learn very fast what not to do, and if not, you were toast. It just so happened to be one of those days for me. This was the daily ritual. "Smoking," is what it is called. For me, well let us just say that I was in very good shape when I left basic training. For the most part, basic training was one of the most lethal challenges that I had ever encountered in my life. The body that was once a child's body will now be transformed into a lean, mean fighting machine. Alternatively, "they," the silent grand majority of the military, called it. It was not fair that the silent majority played your mind like the "old Jedi mind tricks." Reverse psychology was the best of the tricks that could be played on one's mind. It was effective to get the job done, if you did not know it was happening to you.

CHAPTER 3

The Snare

For nine weeks, I suffered in the hot, blistering South Carolina heat, firing in the same foxholes as my predecessor. Long days and nights in the sand and sawdust pits conditioned my mind and body, along with the long days spent marching out to the ranges and then marching back at night. These were the type of "Ruck Marches," which made me think twice about what I had done in the first place. Why in the hell would anyone want to do such a thing to oneself? I learned to deal with the pain which started to take its toll on every inch of my body, and I began feeling a sense of accomplishment for what I had just done, putting a reason to all this torture.

Of course, there were days when I just could not go on anymore, but something inside made me push on, as if I had something to prove to myself. In any event, if you did not, then you were forced to the edge of your wits, and then some. They called it "conditioning," but I say it was just plain, outright pain, or so I thought. Just when I thought I couldn't go anymore, something deep inside of me reached down, picked up the rest of my tired, weak body, and carried me to the end. It was the first part of me that would see the reasoning behind all this agony. I was going through the transformation from the civilian way of thinking to a soldier's way of thinking.

Dear Diary: 1986

I feel strange, not like the kid I once was. Something happened to me during basic training; something out of the ordinary that is not seen, smelled, or heard; something psychological. One minute, I was thinking of going home, and the next, I was thinking of killing on the battlefield. It is strange that I cannot put my finger on what happened. I do remember running to the foxhole at the range as I passed through some trees, and a drill sergeant came out from the middle of nowhere and scared me to death. I remember stopping dead in my tracks and doing nothing. I could not speak or anything, yet I felt the change after my head finally came to. The drill sergeant kept asking me if I was all right, and then I just came to and there I was, standing like a soldier. I never could understand that. I have been told that I snapped, and what I snapped into was a soldier. Nevertheless, like anything else in basic training, I just said, "Yes, drill sergeant." Then I got my butt chewed and ran off to the foxhole to kill a paper target.

Did you ever wonder what happened to you at basic training? Maybe it was me, but those I have talked to about it remember the same thing I do. Something strange seems to take over, as if you are gently forced onto another path. I could feel the transformation happening as this kid inside me stood back, like an out-of-body experience, watching the changes from the inside out. I call this brainwashing, but the army calls this the skills to survive. It is almost as if a switch turned off and another one turned on from a different place and time. I am not sure how or why, but the child that was inside me seemed to transform into a vicious fighting machine that had a gentle, compassionate side to him, but given the chance before me to unleash the wrath of God, I would not hesitate for a second.

In addition to each accomplishment, I felt pride beginning to building up inside of me as each one of us accomplished a task and cheered one another on, pushing one another to finish a given task. It no longer mattered if you hated that person before, it was as if you were all a team. In this case, the team was being built before our very own eyes, and we did not even know it. Anticipation grew in each one of us as graduation drew closer. Nights would close with all of us gathering in the sandpit for boot-shining, as we discussed the failures of some who were dismissed from the now-elite due to family issues, dishonesty, psychological problems, or the showstopper, medical. Some would still cry at night as they laid there in the hard, cardboard bunk with no comfort of home or family and friends to save the day. It has been months now since we last saw our families and friends, as graduation had us stepping onto the parade field, displaying our accomplishments and pride within. Family and friends would not be able to tell this man from the child that once was. Once a misfit and even more a profound misfit; nevertheless, can I just do it on a higher plan of professionalism now? Oh my God, had I just transformed into a savior of the world, running in the gauntlet of challenges as they confronted me. I thought that I was evincible to the world's challenges? Yet, I realized, all too quickly, with a profound roar from the drill instructor, that I was just another number to the eyes of the world, as I remembered all the pain of trials within each one of us as we struggled together throughout basic training. There were all kinds of people coming from all backgrounds and diversities. This was something I was not used to at all. I remember having to choose the wrong side over the right to save my own hide from the beatings. There were those who never showered and would be taken into the shower and literally scrubbed from head to toe with a very stiff brush. There were those who still wet the bed. And then there were those who were able to sleep with their eyes open, standing up while in training. Now that was a sight to see. That kid never graduated, but he had a knack for that kind of stuff. I tend to think he was the smartest one out of all of us. There were some who hid their medical issues from the military, which in turn took some of their lives in the process, but the most profound incident in basic training in all of our lives is when someone snaps. I guess someone snaps, because it is hard to keep an eye on everyone while in the last range of basic training, and the one person you thought had his head together goes into the "Port-a-john" and puts a bullet in his head. When they found him minutes later, it was said that his "K-pot" was lowered on his head. I guess the 5.56 millimeter round does scramble a brain. The truth of the matter is, when he was sent home from basic, they had to have a closed casket funeral.

Dear Diary: 1986

The day has come when I actually accomplished something on my own now. I will be graduating army basic training tomorrow morning, how cool is that? I really felt that I have done something on my own now for a change and didn't let anyone down. I sure hope Dad can come to see me. He would be proud.

I graduated basic training and moved onto the advance individual training for my specific MOS. For those who will never understand military terminology, this means "military occupational specialty." My specialty, or job, in the military was, combat medical specialists, or "91A," in short. I figured that, since I was never really popular with anyone in my younger years, I would just go to the extreme lengths to finding a great woman to put up with my shit for the rest of my life, and what better place to pick a woman than the medical field. Nurses are hot, if you think about it. They look so hot in short, white dresses that you can practically see through, or in their white, see-through pants. I spent most of the time in classes and practicing for the gauntlet of exams that were scheduled every week. After passing the majority of tests that were given, I was awarded the job title of combat medic; a noble title that was worth having. Still, my heart just did not seem to be there with the medical corps, as I had planned it in the beginning.

I went home for Christmas vacation before I was to be shipped out to Germany. Before I left on the bus, Walter, my buddy from basic training, who had followed me into the medical corps, ran up to me and told me of several openings in the military police corps. It did not take much for him to jar my mind and give me the skinny on the job description: young, wild, and traveling to exotic places and given the authority to carry a gun and a badge. Wow, who could ask for more then that? It didn't take long for Walter and me to run to the retention office to have orders transferring the both of us to the military-police side of the house. With that in my pocket, I boarded the bus for home and took my vacation in peace. Something inside felt right, for once in my life. Something inside said that I would be going places and doing a great deal of good things for my country. Yet my experiences were just beginning for my long tour of duty.

After my vacation, I was on orders for Ft. McClellan, Alabama, for military-police school. It was the most exciting thing that could be happening to me. Greeted by the drill instructors this time was somewhat tame compared to basic training. Here, they actually allowed you to have some freedom to go and do what you wanted, but still had the restrictions of the "mother," if you get my drift.

The challenges became even greater as the world was putting their trust in me as one of the youngest military policemen on their block. It is amazing how the world can grant so much trust to those that do not even know anything about wiping their own noses by offering them a gun and badge and having them police the world's terror in battle. This was my ticket to death if I was not careful, yet I was on top of the world. Military-police school almost emulated basic training, with the exception of learning paperwork, police tactics, and other tiring police things. Marching to the ranges and doing combat battlefield movements was where I wanted to be. Infantry basic was okay, but in the military police corps, you got to see and do more then your average Joe in the field. The military police train to be the standard, and so we make the standards, because we are the standard-setters for the rest of the military. Did you get that one? Well, I did, and that is all that matters now. Basically, we are bad assess on caffeine, for sure. Learning the laws is where most soldiers fail out of the course, but for me, that was second nature. It was as if I were supposed to be a lawman. However, for the most part, it is easy to do. You do have to have some form of common sense to be a cop, and you have to want to help others. Those others can be anyone, even the ones who call you to the enemy. You cannot just shoot and ask questions later, like you see on television. It is not like that at all. The military police corps has a very prestigious history, as every graduate of the military police corps will learn; and with that said, I finally made it myself.

Dear Diary: 1986-1987

Life sure has chanced for me in the past year, from being a snot-nosed kid, to being a military policeman. It is amazing how life tends to trick you into things you never thought you would be doing. I went from the tortures of a mad childhood to being a trained killer of the cold war era, well that is something to speak for in itself. There are many who will play the pity-me act throughout the years, but as I go through my career, but I will try my best to be better than that. I will strive to be somebody, and not just be another Joe in the army. Diary, I will keep you posted as my career takes shape. Boy, Dad and Mom would truly be proud if they could only see me now. I finally made something of myself.

The successful completion of military-police school seemed to have granted me a key to the world. It became obvious to me as I completed the next task that another would open up, and I was offered to the wolves again, but only in the most subtle of ways. In a few short months, I had done a vast amount of growing inside, and I opened doors to the world and to the next life that would bestow itself upon me for the next half-plus century of my life. There was a short stay of block leave back home in Arizona again, and then I was on orders for Germany. Dad was proud of me for all that I had accomplished in such a short period of time. Now he could see the new person that had become "his little soldier boy." This young, snot-nosed kid that would never amount to anything had transformed into a real man now. You know: the young kid who has never even been out of the state of Arizona was now on his way to another county. Even though the visit was well worth the stay, something inside of me was letting go of the family that needed me so much. I felt as if the memories of the past were fading away with every passing minute, yet it still hung around like a tree snake waiting for me to pass underneath, only to be bitten by the memories that would now haunt me forever.

Do not get me wrong; the memories of the past were not at all that bad, but like any other kid's life, it had its times between good and bad. Only now, this grown young man had to explain to his father that he was going to another country and would not be around as I am now. I love and cherish my dad more then life itself, but I somehow needed to tell him that I need the space to grow and see the vast world out there. Let us just say I could not bring myself to do it. I tried to look into my father's eyes, which burned deep down inside as he stopped and listened to me for once. All the years of pain that I had seen in his eyes over my years of growing up and all that we have been through came back in seconds as I stared into my fathers eyes. I tried to set his mind at ease by telling him about all the training I had received and the vast knowledge base that I had now. It did not seem to comfort him enough to allow his son to go away, but it was something that had to happen. I needed him to let go, just enough to start letting me have a life of my own. After hours of talking Dad seemed amazed that I had accomplished so much, and that it did not cost him, or anyone else, anything. His once -dreamer was now a real-life dream-maker. I remember watching myself in the mirror, singing to Freddy Fender records, wearing my bell-bottom jeans and a corduroy shirt, with high-heeled platform boots, and thinking that one day I would get my break and make it big on the circuit. This was very different from the days of singing. "Dad, I made it," I said to him as we sat at the kitchen table eating lunch. The fears seemed to have lifted, and the look in his eyes revealed his relief that his son has made something of himself. The typical father who worried about his children and only wanted what was best for them was now a thing of the past. You try to do what is right and raise your children to be the best. Some make it, and others do not, but you still strive to give them the best. What more could any parent ask for than to see their child succeed in life? My father, to me, is the center of my life. Without the huge sacrifices and pain that he had to go through to raise us kids to where we were now, I would not be saying thank you at that very time. Life tore at my father's heart after the death of a wife, two divorces, a house fire, a torn family, and losing it all repeatedly. Seeing this from a child's perspective was not what any child should grow up with, but it happens daily to thousands. There does come a time when the child inside has to set aside time to allow myself to be a kid again. I prayed for the best, and received what was given to me. Granted, not all of my childhood was bad, but there are things that I wish I could change.

CHAPTER 4
The Trip

Dear Diary: 1987

Hello again, diary. I am scared to death. I am going to a place I have never been. I am leaving home, and not to mention, my homeland for another land, Germany. What will happen to me? Will I be captured as a prisoner like in the old World War II movies? I am truly scared for my life that I will be captured, tortured, and then killed. The looks from all the civilians...they all look at me as if I am a criminal, killer, or something. I think I am going to go to sleep right now on the plane. I know I won't, but I can sure try.

My nerves began to churn inside as I prepared my mind for the trip of a lifetime. Isn't it amazing how everyone seems to be a subject-matter expert for something you are about to do? They love to sound so honorable as they discuss their happenings when they were there moments before you, making the very same mistakes; emphasizing the importance of everything, you should and should not do, yet they made the same mistakes. I guess this is the way society learns from its mistakes, or at least some of us do. I would take some of it and run with it, but the rest would easily be tossed to the side, and I could be ignoring the possibilities that were laid before me by my peers. Could this be the wrong choice that I am making? Maybe it is the right choice. Maybe they want to lead me astray so that they can take the credit for themselves. I am not sure, and that is what so much fun about being yourself. No one can take that from you as you make the decisions on your own and go with your gut feelings. These are the choices in life, and that is what you have to live with. Wrong, right, or indifferent; these are your choices, and yours alone.

I quickly determined that the best thing was to wait until I got there and make that determination for myself. That's not such a bad idea, if you think about it. The mysteries of the world were in my grasp, and I loved it. The really cool part of this job is when you are in the airport and in Class-A's, and of my first experience with all the expressions on the faces of those who despised the baby killers of the world, mixed with the sultry looks from the young girls who admire a man in uniform; you know the ones: the too-proud-and-still-Daddy's-little girls who had nothing better to do than toy with your mind as you spent the rest of your life thinking about where life would take them. I remember thinking of that one look they gave me and wondering if I had what it takes to make them just go nuts over me. It's typical to most, but it is a girl thing. I think they take the girls off to the side and teach them this stuff in school. I can just see it now: a book called, *The Many Ways to Torture a Man*. For me, sitting and daydreaming about sex was a daily thing for a loner, pondering what I would do and how I would treat them. That's enough said for the life of a nerd. A few hours later, I found myself dreaming myself to sleep with a smile on my face after catching the attention of the very sexy airline stewardess who allowed me to sneak a peak up her already-short skirt as she attempted to squeeze into those pathetic foldaway seats. It was even better as I puffed out my chest, which was really a gasp for air after seeing the long, sexy legs of a newly trained, well-endowed young stewardess as she adjusted her legs, giving me a peepshow better then that of a topless club.

Just when you think you have her in the palm of your hand, the unthinkable happens. A male steward would emerge from around the corner, ruining the image you just had embedded in your collective mind for the rest of your natural born life. You know the ones that try to look tough; the epitome of showing off, but in reality, are actually homosexual? At least that is the way they project themselves to me; all nice and pretty for the present company. In addition, just to rub it in one more time, when it came time for the meal to be served, the one and only hot babe you thought you were going to be served by was on reserve for the upper-class section, only. Oh no, you are stuck with the want-to-be-tough guy or what's even worse, the old hag who sat up front and treated you like you did not even exist to the rest of the world. It was all I could do to sit quietly in this sardine can, trying hard not to make it obvious that I wanted the girl of my dreams to serve me instead. I think they do the switch on you just to tease you into thinking you have it all, then the world's biggest letdown hits you square in the face. They give you that simple smile and look away as they ignore your feeble existence, right after passing you the tiny bag of peanuts with only three nuts inside and a side-order drink, just enough to wet your tongue. Now call me a pervert, but hasn't this happen all too many times to you? I think so. What male doesn't think of what he would do with that hot stewardess in the airplane's bathroom?

After a long, grueling flight of twenty-three hours, my arrival in Germany was a welcome all on its own. I had to pee so badly that I could fill a ten-liter bottle. I never thought, in my wildest dreams, that I would travel to new and exotic places of the world, and Germany in the year 1987 was a strange world to a foreigner like me. But the feeling of home came over me as I was greeted with open arms. At first, I did not know what to think until I was greeted again and again, as the German nationals spoke in their native tongue while using my name.

I felt like a king in this place, as if I were a VIP to those who followed behind me. New sounds mixing with the view of a new place flooded my senses. The smell of fresh danishes being baked in the airport bakery tantalized my taste buds, enticing me to go inside and buy as many as I could eat in one sitting. I had only seen images of European woman on the television, but face to face, I would have never believed that European woman were so beautiful. The German police walked the beat in the airport halls en masse, carrying Uzi machine guns and Lugar pistols. The K-9 unit handlers struggle to hold back their German Shepard sentry dogs that as they sniffed everything within sight. Yes, the customs were truly different here, and they gave new meaning to the stories on the news about the cold war, which I was very much a part of. Seeing the differences in freedoms that we, as Americans, have taken for granted, truly slapped me hard in the face as I saw and felt the restrictions imposed on society here. This was even the simplest of things, such as freedom of movement. Yes, you could move around, but the feeling that everyone was watching you or even taking your picture was in the back of your mind all the time. The everyday person you dealt with could turn out to be the enemy, so it was no wonder that reality for me set in quickly as I started to deal with people. It seemed as though everyone was a spy, and you were the enemy. Yes, customs here were definitely different than what I was accustomed to.

With the Berlin Wall still up, I could feel the hate rain upon the soldiers in green as we passed the normal populist within the halls of the baggage claim. The static of squawking in their native tongue as I stood there with my fellow soldier brother an, snapped at my ears. I bit my tongue as I listened to the lewd comments that lashed out at the likes of our kind being in their country. It did not seem to be as bad as everyone had talked about, but it was enough for me to comment below my breath about those that did speak out at us. As I passed them, they would see my nameplate, and I would watch their change in expression to puzzlement about such as name as mine, employed in such a country.

So here I was in Germany, thousands of miles away from home, and life's true experiences began to happen all around me. I spent the majority of my off time traveling throughout the Eastern and Western Blocks of Europe. My time there was amazing, compared to anything that I have ever done in this life. Just about every morning before work-call formation, I would go across the quad to the German canteen to get a cup of Turkish coffee and a schnitzel. What a way to start a day of freezing snow and cold in the motor pool, while working on the jeep. You tease the rest with your ability to get something to wake you up, and you feed yourself before you go to work. Most of the day was spent fixing the brakes that we did not get fixed the day before. The majority of the soldiers "fucked off" the workday as a few of us worked our asses off. Now, being that I was one of the lowest on the food chain, I was stuck doing most of the work. If you think about it, though, it actually helped me in a good way and worked to my advantage. Think of it like this: there are those who pretend, and then there are those of us who act on what we know. By learning how to work on the engines, radios, and other equipment, it became evident that just about everyone needed me when something went wrong. The glory of this is that you have the right now to pick and choose what you would and would not do and for whom. To make the time pass, I merely listened to all the other conversations as the other soldiers discussed their plans for weekends to come. It was amazing how most of them only wanted to go to the bar, or even stay in and do nothing. I chose to go to the castles and spend an entire weekend walking the steps that warriors walked before me while defending the castle and the townspeople within the walls. From the watchtowers that extended high into the sky, I peered over lush green prairie land and catch sight of miles of vineyards that produces thousands of bottles of the finest wines in the world. The crisp, clean, and cool wind blew past my face and whistled in my ears, such a peaceful way to take in the sights of ruins. The sounds alone when you close your eyes take you to another place in time, when the renaissance ruled the lands here, as beautiful women in large lace gowns waited for the rescue of a knight in metal clothing, only to leave them in the night, running off to battle. Kings and queens ruled the lands for all, and mankind lived and died by the sword.

The other sites I enjoyed visiting were the nude beaches; yes, a nude beach is what I said. Going to them did not seem to bother me too much, as I participated in the nude sun bathing and swimming myself. It just seemed natural for me, and it was a way to get away from the soldiers from time to time. The body is a beautiful thing, and if you don't like yourself for who you are, then how can you like anyone else? I just learned, over time, to become more open-minded about life and the experiences within it. Girls were not a fair part of my life right now, so seeing them nude was just another thing. Yes, there were times when I stared a little too long, but I was in a new country, I was having fun, and it was cool. Now don't get me wrong; I had many friends that were girls. Moreover, they knew that I did not want anything from them, so going to the nude beaches was the perfect place where I could go to get away from the military and blend in with the majority. Now, for those that think I had lost my mind, I will set that straight for you now: like any man, I thought about it, and yes, it was very tempting, having several very hot girls in front of you as you talked away, and all you could do was stare at their tight, golden bodies as they baked in the hot sun; but that was not what I was there for. I fit in, and that was the nice part. In this case, I made many friends and partied with a butt load of very hot chicks.

Moving on to the more exciting things to do in Germany, here is an example of just two things that are necessary for anyone who goes to Germany. One is the Christmas-fest in December. They make the best "Glue-Vine," which is better than any wine or hard liquor. The more you drink, the worse you get. Nevertheless, it tastes so darned good. Of course, the world-famous schnitzel is a must. Just before you leave the streets for the day and head for the bed, do not forget to take along some world-famous chocolate, in case you wake up in the middle of the night and need a snack. This is where I got my chocolate addiction, and I am proud of it, thank you very much! But all the lights and the little trinkets that are for sale in the booths are really a sight to see.

Second, if you are a true party animal, then you must go to the Oktoberfest. This is the party of a lifetime, where the party goes all day and night and goes on and on and on. Need I say more? However, do not drink too much while eating pizza then go on the amusement-park rides, especially the ones that turn you upside down. Everything you have had in you comes back out in a really bad and forceful way, which is not that bad if you are a hardcore drinker. This means you have more room for beer and food. However, for those who cannot handle the big parties, there are always the tours to the crystal and chocolate factories. I preferred to do them all: The Volk's Fests, crystal and chocolate factories, and all the street sales throughout the country. In the total reality of it all, Germans are some party-hungry people, and I was proud to have known them, because they really know how to throw a party.

Dear Diary: December 1987

I feel like one of the double agents right out of the spy movies. I feel very strange over here. Everyone is so touchy about everything. You cannot even say "Boo" without someone wanting to turn you in or shoot you. The mystery is so neat. It seems sexy and romantic, in a way, that the cold war era is about to end, and Germany will be free; yet the spy mystery is still very much alive and well. I cannot absorb it all fast enough.

So, now that I am the only one in my immediate family who has gone overseas traveling all over the Eastern and Western Blocs of Europe, I can expect to be called the leading authority on Germany. "Not in this lifetime;" but what is really cool about this whole thing was that I was paid for doing all of this. It was not a bad deal, but in some cases, the weak minded have to have Mommy and Daddy right next to them, because they can't do it on their own, or they are just too dead set on being lazy for the rest of their natural-born lives, while I took the time to do something with myself. And that is why you always hear the same thing from the old friends you knew back in grade school. "Gosh, you did a lot in your short time after high school." Well yeah! I just chose not to be a bump on a log and become a college, snot-nosed asshole like the rest and get a half-witted salary-paying job from which they would eventually be laid off anyway. Instead, I went around the world, saw a great deal and did a lot of really cool things. Oh, and all you hard-earning taxpayers paid for it all for me. I like that.

Thanks!

Do I endorse joining the military? Sure, if you like getting away from everyone and everything and living the hard life of hot and cold weather, and playing in the mud and rain, with every imaginable bug known to man. In addition, you are away from the ones you love for practically the rest of the time you are in the military, which in my case, felt like a prison sentence. However, in reality, it is not all that bad. Here are just some of the perks that go with the job: you get to travel anywhere in the world at the expense of our great nation; you are like a regular frigging James Bond, and you have a license to kill anyone, anywhere in the world, within reason, of course. I do not want you to get the wrong impression and then go out and start killing people. That is just wrong. For all you nut cases out there, don't take this literally. You are a professional and are trained to kill, but only if necessary. You get practically free medical and dental. You are fed pretty good meals. They give you a place you can call your own for the little time you are there. You get to travel throughout the world, free or practically free, all the time. If you think about it hard, remember back to the days when you were a kid and playing cops and robbers or cowboys and Indians. Well, if you use the same concept, then you will be right at home. Each day is different, and you get to be a part of the real adventure. Moreover, if you keep your nose clean, you even get to keep your paycheck and rank.

Anyway, there are so many things to see and do while you are in the military that your lifetime could not cover it all. I have done so much in the short time I have been in the military that I have almost filled up my life with memories. Nevertheless, it still cannot fill the void that had been taken from me as I left my loved ones behind and ran off into the night to fight someone else's war for them. For the most part, I am privileged to have all that I do. I have worked hard for it all, and I have enjoyed a grand majority of what I have done, but do not get me wrong; there were bad times for me, as well. I try not to let that get to me as much, yet the void will be there as long as it takes to find myself again.

If I had to pick a favorite place out of all that I have seen and done throughout my time in the service, it would have to be my tours in Germany. The different coffees, food, and chocolate all had their own way of drawing you into the store to buy them. The castles, scenery, and many countries where I have been all have their own secret place in my heart; each different in smell, sight, and sound. Granted, most of the places are old, war-torn countries, and the structures are mangled, yet the culture seemed to replace the structure as it nurtured itself back to standing health within my eyes as I envisioned that place as it once was. The mere remnants of the structures are enough to show off their true history. I would say, for the most part, that I connected with the culture and its ways when I was there. Maybe it has to do with the linage that I have there. Who knows? So I say again, can it be all that bad? I say no, and we all need a little humbling every now and then. Get out and see the world. You live in it, so why not see it?

A small piece of me did do some work, too, while I stayed in Germany.

Dear Diary: November 1987

The unit has asked me to represent them in the next "French Commando Entrainment" Competition in France. Being the fitness stud and adventurous person that I am, I think I will take the honors and show myself off to the world. I have already showed that I have what it takes to shoot better then the rest. I will be leaving in two days for the French Alps. What a place to go, huh? Oh, and I guess this makes me a badass now, huh? Well, not likely, but I can at least shoot straight, and then if I didn't get you the first time, then I know how to sneak up on you and get you. Nevertheless, it was fun and I learned something new.

I was proud to be just one of the thirty-three lucky soldiers to represent the unit and the United States military as a whole when I asked to attend the "French Commando School," in France, for the annual French/American joint training. This is where I was tested for the skills to do what others would never dream of doing. Earning my "French Commando Entrainment Badge" was probably one of the best things that had ever happened to me. I never thought I had it in me to become a commando, but I did. Nevertheless, like any young stud, I took myself to newer heights within the world. I then went on and won the "Gold German Koblenz (Schutzen-Schnur), in 1994. That was a long year of getting to know different weapons and traditions with weapons. I think, in all, I memorized over 249 different weapons systems. That's a lot to speak of, but if you stop to think about it, 249 is not even close to what the special forces and all the other branches get to play with. I was just scratching the surface. Many other schools were attended to the benefit of the unit and the military, but where I gained my vast knowledge, was the entire stay within the military as a whole. Still, Germany had its grips on me. I was totally fascinated with the barracks where I stayed, which still had the German SS swastikas on the stair casings of each floor as you walked through the building. It was all a part of the cold war of course. It became second nature for me to search high and low for the relics of the past within the very dorm that I now reside in. Every morning, I would get up early enough before formation to go to the German cantina just across the courtyard. There was a very nice old man and woman who worked the counter who seemed to had been left over from the war. They must have had photographic memories, because I ordered a large Turkish coffee and a Bratwurst at the same time every morning. They must have memorized my footsteps as I came down the old concrete steps to the cellar door, because they had my items ready as I walked in the door. After the first year, for some reason, I didn't have to pay for the items anymore. They kept saying "You no pay anymore. Go, and be happy." They had a very pretty daughter who came in from time to time, but she was already spoken for. Their son had been killed in a car accident, and it amazed me, after seeing the photo, that I looked somewhat like the young chap. Maybe they adopted me as their son without me knowing, but they always did take care of me.

Dear Dairy: 1987

I must have the worst luck in the world. I just ended up back in the German hospital after having my head split wide open by a Turkish nationalist hitting me in the back of my skull and laying me out for the count. I do recall seeing the look of surprise on the face of the German police officer just before I was hit. I do not remember anything after that. The Germans seem to have a great sense of humor as they keep telling jokes in the lobby outside my room. The best part was when they came in the room, and I spoke to them in German. The look on their faces after they found out I understood every word they said; now that was funny. It seems to be that I am accident prone. Here, I am the only badass to be accident prone and I lying up in the hospital bed more then any soldier in history. I just do not get it, man.

Touring the old German Castles gave me a sense of the luxury of living that came with it. I felt the sense of closeness as I walked the halls of the wealthy, down to the peasants; from the peasants to those jailed within the walls of the castle. The beautiful gardens that once graced the eyes of only the wealthy now showed their true colors to the world and all who dared to come within its grasp. The winding cobblestone streets that lead to the high-rise estate were just big enough for one small car and perfectly weathered with time. It is such a pity that it is all going to waste as time takes its toll on that which we do not take care of.

Dear Diary: 1988

I cannot sleep tonight. I just got in from shift, and it was a bad one. I had to go to a traffic accident, where a mother and child went head on with a semi truck. The strange thing was that the mother did not have a scratch on her, but was covered in blood. I cannot get over the look on the dead infant's face as it dropped out of the wreckage and onto the car floor as the fire department pulled with the Jaws of Life. Dead as it was, it still looked deep into my soul and stained my mind forever. Every time I close my eyes, I see it looking back at me. The screams from the mother pierce my eardrums to the core…Sorry I had to go throw up again. I have been doing that a lot since the accident. I need to go lay down.

CHAPTER 5

The Cold War Scare

My typical explanation of Germany, seen through the eyes of millions on the boob tube, and portrayed in the old movies of World War One and Two, had me thinking of Gingerbread Houses and your typical cold-war era, snow-covered world of hate and disarray. To my astonishment, the television is not all that it is cracked up to be when establishing a basis for the way it truly is over there.

It was early in the morning when the death horns rang throughout the land, waking me up before the alarm clock. Its ear-piercing noise scrambled my dreams, awakening me to the disturbing yelling of people in the hallway outside my barracks door, and was followed by a sudden pounding on the solid door that secured me in my dungeon with the loud noises echoing throughout the room. The person on the other side of the door reminded me of a bad dream where I would hide under the covers as the door from my closet rasped open in anticipation of loud noises that would never come. In reality, it was only a gust of wind from the air-conditioning unit that forced it open, but that is not what your mind keeps telling you as it is happening. It is as if something were going to jump out and get you, but it never does. Instead, you become so tired of staring at the door and the darkness behind it, knowing that nothing is really there, you continue to stare until you fall asleep, leaving your mind empty in the morning. Years later, you laugh at the position you woke up in and remembered how dorky you looked.

I pried my lazy body from the warmth of the sheets and opened the door slowly. I did not even have a chance to get the door one-quarter of the way open when my team leader popped his head in and rattled off something that for the life of me I will never remember. All I heard was, "Plaaahhh," as he ran off to the next door. After being scared half to hell with the jolts of doors slamming shut, the sounds of people banging on doors, the death horn, and troops running up and down the hallway; this day was determined to be a bad day for me, and it had not started yet. All within the seconds that my team leader popped in the door and I closed the door to get dressed, the platoon sergeant opened the door and began yelling the same instructions that my team leader yelled out to everyone.

Now, correct me if I am wrong, but I thought there was something that had to do with knocking in this game. I guess not, if you are at the top. Then, I guess that is where I want to be. Again, I acknowledged him and then walked to the door to close it after the platoon sergeant ever-so-nicely left it open. Don't you just hate those types; the ones who were born in the barn and feel that they don't have to do anything but be waited on. That was how I felt at that time and place. I guess they never figured out how to close a door, but I think it is part of the asshole syndrome that comes with being at the top of the food chain. I could be wrong. I just don't get it.

I managed to get dressed and work my way down to the arms room, where everyone was being assigned weapons and live ammunition. I quickly received my assigned weapon, the

M2 .50-caliber machine gun and two cans of ammunition. The assistant gunner helped carry my weapon and boxes of ammunition to the holding area in the back of the building. Once I reached the holding area, which was surrounded by concertina wire and an armed guard on either end of the outside fence, we all mustered for the formation where we would finally be told what the heck was going on. The commander approached the front of the formation and addressed us all with the surprise of a lifetime.

"The United States European Command was informed that there was a massing of enemy troops to the north, and it is our mission to go to the area and see what their intentions are. We are the quick-reaction force for the region, and the task of the quick-reaction force is to be the first responders to anything that might be posing a threat to our north. Now, our mission is to make contact, observe, and report back to the force that would be coming after us to spank that ass, should the need find itself."

Believe what you want, but I was there. I was too new to the army to know what this all meant, and I started getting more and more frightened as the sergeants marched us all to the motor pool. As we marched down the street to the motor pool, vehicles that were traveling along our route halted on the shoulder of the road to try catching a glimpse of the speed bumps that would be used before they would go to battle. Our vehicles lined the roadway in march order as we prepared to travel to our doom. Soldiers running around were stopping and giving way to the large formation that was coming through. The looks on the faces of all of them were of empathy and trepidation. It was as if they know we were not coming back, and as if they were paying their last respects to the elite ones who were to be the very first to face the enemy in years. The threat was very real to the cold-war region, and the world knew it. I remember seeing the news media was stopped at the front gates of the base as we turned into the motor pool. Soldiers from across the quad were halting to see the massive formation of military police marching to their death. For once in my life, I was scared, and the frigid, cold wind that chilled me to the bone didn't seem to bother me anymore. The only thing that penetrated my mind was the crunching of the six-inch deep, hard, white snow that laid on the cold ground beneath my feet as I made my way to the motor pool. The formation stopped, and we were all given instruction to load up quickly and get ready to depart the area immediately and go to the staging area. A tiny jeep was all that stood between my enemy and me. There was no top to hold in the heat, and obviously no cover from the enemy. The front gates of the base opened as our convoy exited. Distant sounds of track vehicles starting up and moving into position made this war that much more of a reality. I became calm as I saw behind our convoy; a massing of Abrams tanks. That was a sight to see, and for the enemy it was a sight to be reckoned with. I placed inside myself the anger that was building up alongside the fear that stood proudly. As reality sets in, it is amazing how all the training you learned in the past catches up to you so quickly.

I turned and faced front, staring down the road towards the enemy. The funny thing is it was nothing like this in training. Just then, my memories came back to me. Could this be what I had been dreaming about all these years? Was this the reason I had such a huge fascination with those damn green toy soldiers when I was younger; you know, the ones that came in the tin can of about five hundred to a thousand that you could get for only five dollars at K-Mart? And the more you had, the better the wars were. Heck, GI Joe didn't have what these guys had. It even came with a jeeps, tanks, jet airplanes, walls, flags, concertina wire, and a command post. I started to reminisce back to those days when I would lie on the floor in the front living room of our old-run down doublewide trailer and play with them for hours, making mock wars as I watched John Wayne movies, *Hogan's Heroes*, and *Gilligan's Island*. There were even times when I woke up the next morning on the floor to morning cartoons, like *Sesame Street*, and *The Electric Company*.; you know, those basic shows that never amounted to anything, or so they say. The cartoons on today are more violent than any show that was on before. Moreover, the people at the top wonder why kids are doing what they are nowadays, with all the senseless killings schools and kids going to jail at younger ages. But for right now, the battle that I had left the night before was still in full force, right where I had left it, under the television stand, the coffee table, and practically the entire living-room floor.

Let me tell you, it was no picnic being the gunner on the back end of a jeep, especially in the dead of winter, as the bitter cold burned through my field jacket, straight to my bones. Miles passed as I stood, shivering, behind the steel-mounted .50-caliber machine gun, with my hands frozen in a hard grip to the weapon. My cheeks were frozen and bright red from the windburn that scorched my face as we raced down the autobahn.

My body literally froze into position as the raggedy old jeep traveled down the autobahn. Cold wind spanked my face as my fingers froze to the .50-caliber machine gun that extended almost past the front end of the jeep. White snow covered the ground in every direction in which I attempted to look. At times, I feared turning my head for the fear that the cold had frozen my neck so much that it would break like glass if I attempted to turn it. The sun didn't seem to want to come out, and I soon found that in the wee hours of the morning that as the sun was coming up, the colder it would get, until the sun fully rises in the sky to warm the earth. As the convoy stopped for a moment's rest, soldiers as far as the eye could see were peeling themselves from gunners' platforms. The NCOs did the normal thing for their job status: They started yelling again, and giving times for departure and where we were allowed to go. I was having a hard time just prying my frozen hands from the gun. My fingers had frozen to the metal on the trigger. The platoon leader was concerned that I was going to have frostbite because I couldn't straighten my fingers or get the ice-covered glove off of my hands once they pried my hands from the weapon. I must have some luck, because it was not too much longer when the sun had popped up over the mountains and started to warm everything up. The snow didn't melt, but I could feel my hands soon after they were pulled from the weapon.

Day started to break over the mountaintops as the weather began to get even colder. After about five straight hours of traveling, the convoy pulled over into a rest stop. As we found our spot in the pooling area, the reverberating sounds of the track-armored vehicles that followed closely behind us engrossed me. There were no places for the tracks in the pooling area, so they were clanking and whining as they slowly came to a halt along the autobahn. After about ten minutes of trying to pry my fingers off the weapon. I was able to release it and get down from the mount to go and take a piss. The strangest thing came over me as I looked around. I noticed that there were no civilians around. I also noticed the same thing as we were traveling down the autobahn, but didn't notice until now. Have you ever gotten that cold chill down your spine that something is wrong? I am not talking about the cold weather that was trying to turn me into a popsicle. I was told of this type of thing happening in the past, during World War II. There were some people out on the road, but the majority seemed to have been swallowed up by the cobblestone walkways and gingerbread houses. The fear of the host nation's people stared at us in disbelief as the movement awakened them, as though the post-cold war was starting all over again. All I could think about at this point was an Arizona summer, and how I would have liked to be there right about now. There, at one of the many stops along the way before we reached the border, soldiers piled out of jeeps, trucks, and tracks; trying to get in that one smoke they didn't get to have earlier, and warming up their bodies with the exhaust from the tailpipes of the jeeps, trucks, and tracks. We all looked like a New York, South Central; winter ghetto convention. Soldiers stood around the one and only fifty-gallon barrel drum, trying to warm up with the only paper left to burn for ten thousand miles. In this case, it was our vehicles that kept us all alive. But as the best was getting to all of us, it wasn't long before the sergeants were yelling for the movement to get going and calling everyone back as the convoy commenced to slowly creep down the autobahn once more. The sun was high in the sky, and the day was turning out to be fairly nice. I was not as cold as I was earlier. A calming sort of peace came over me as the border appeared in the distance. As we were nearing the border, radio traffic flooded the airwaves. The track vehicles that were following us peeled off into the tree line and began moving around the formations of trucks and jeeps on the roadway. Attack helicopters raced over our heads to spot the enemy before they can get any closer.

The platoon leaders and sergeants began yelling orders to move up into position. Not too far over a small hillside stood soldiers in white uniforms. Others laid in the white snow, camouflaging them from the view of any other person. In the distance were trucks, personnel carriers, and tanks, including one of the most deadly in the world, the T-72 Russian tank. Tension was so thick that you could cut it with a knife. Both sides stood, staring at each other and sizing up the others' strengths and weaknesses with their egos. As a KA-50 Black Shark attack helicopter emerged from behind the hill, I started to feel a little uneasy, as the pilot stared the others and me down. By the time I would even get off one round, the gun ship would have killed me ten times over. I think the lot of us were just amazed at the sheer size of the gunship that hovered in the air over the treetops, just waiting for the order to pounce on this upcoming superpower.

Tensions continued to build up on both sides as tanks and ground forces pushed forward to the front line of battle. That feeling of being a bad ass was now swelling up inside me, as if nothing could kick our powerful collective asses, but of course that is what being a superpower is all about. One aspect is showing the enemy that you have no fear of them at all and are willing to die for a cause, and the other is bluffing so well that they back down. There are many factors involved in battle, but those are the two that I know right now, and I am sure that wars to come will show me more.

While facing down the enemy that should not have come this far, that little bit of strength was quickly diminished as another massive KA-50 Black Shark attack helicopter appeared over the trees. Its enormous size and weapons payload was enough to impress even little-old me. Our very own attack helicopters, the AH-1S Bell Cobra, zoomed in to take up positions in the airspace within the formation, calling their bluff, and ready to pounce when needed. Our helicopter paled in comparison to the enormous killing machine that hovered almost directly to my front. I had no choice but to lock my machine gun on the helicopter and pray he didn't get the first shot off; not that I would have been able to do anything, but I would at least be standing up and dying like any proud American would. That is just the patriot in me.

Have you ever gotten that feeling in your stomach like something bad was just going to happen; you know, the one that tells your mind there is nothing you can do about it either; so just suck it up and die like a man? As the clock ticked away, of course, which seemed like forever, you could hear pins fall in the snow as the noises just seemed to go away, and tunnel vision took over. The noise in my ears was so loud that it drowned itself out. Could this be it? Could this be the last thing I would remember in my life as the bullets impacted my body, shredding me into little pieces, leaving me in the cold, white snow, with my blood dripping over the pure, white ice, as if to be colored flavoring of a snow cone? My hands tensed, and I began to feel a change in the air as a soldier from the other side walked to the battle line and stopped short of crossing over. Minutes later, our commander went to the battle line to meet the soldier. The two of them talked, or they seemed to talk. Just then, another soldier approached the line, and then another. It was like a regular hand-shaking party. I said to myself, "Why don't we just break out the cheese and champagne, then kiss and make up?" As stupid as it seemed, all the hand shaking made me sick to my stomach. There is nothing like saying thanks to the S.O.B. that you are about to kill or be killed by.

Again, the lines of traffic on the radio chatted away, only this time, they was calling in for landlines of communication. Both sides talked more and more, and the soldiers lying in the snow were turning into popsicles. I watched as both sides passed cigarettes in place of cigars. I presume that the cigars were too frozen to be smoked right now, like their soldiers on the ground. It is amazing how the commanders seemed to forge their soldiers that make them look good when it comes to the real deal. Maybe I was already dead, and I was just dreaming all of this. My heart was still pounding from when this had all started. So here we were, on the brink of full-scale war, while both sides are smoking and joking together before the battle with the lower peons on the totem pole freezing our collective asses off, while they took all the glory. They were probably talking about who was going to pay for the beer later at the club, as I heard some of the soldiers talking about in the motor pool on a daily basis. I kept saying to myself that this had to be the dumbest war ever. Of course, with me just being a new soldier, I was only allowed to sit and wait for the verdict and trust in the commander's decisions to either to go to battle or not. I sat quietly and tried to place myself in their shoes as I thought of the times when I was the commander of the green army toys I used to play with all the time, and how I had positioned my troops for a decisive attack on the enemy. Strangely, this was the same formation that I used to put my troops in. The wait continued on as the masterminds talked it out, and Mother Nature took care of the rest of us. Bitter cold and wet snow froze most of us in place. Soldiers lying on the ground were now frozen in place from what little heat they did have melting the snow beneath them, freezing their clothing to the ground. If they wanted to get up, they couldn't, because the heat from their body had melted the snow beneath them, making them stick to the ground as a blanket of snow lightly covered them like a blanket. The wind began to pick up, and a new day in the era of warfare came to pass. The commanders were now returning to their vehicles and rounding up their troops for a move out to their home bases. As the sergeants called for the troops to rally in formation, I chuckled as I watched soldiers on the ground trying to peel themselves from their potential frozen grave. One soldier had to take off his pants in order to get up off the ground, leaving them in place. His body heat had frozen them to the ground where he was lying. As the soldiers policed themselves up, the commanders walked the boundary lines that were covered by the snow. It appeared that Mother Nature did her job right by covering the boundary markers from the East to West. It appeared that the enemy was already on our side of the border. Something inside was telling me that this would not be the last time we would see them.

The journey back to the base seemed short, compared to the trip up to the battle line. There were some spectators who hissed at us as our huge tanks, trucks, and other wheeled vehicles passed. What could you expect from cold-war victims though? The arrogance inside me smirked back at them as I went over in my head the reasons why we are here in their country. If America wasn't here, God only knows what would still be going on in this country, or if there would even be a country. I smiled inside as I watched the changing of time pass before me.

Dear Diary: 1988

It is good to be back in the barracks again. I am sorry I have not written in so long. The past few months have been very frightening to me. I have not really left the barracks for much of anything. After the brief ordeal with the enemy, I have a new respect for the world and life as well, mainly my own. The things I have seen, and that which has happened to me has given me a new respect for life. First, there was the breach of borderlines with the East Germans or Czechoslovakians. Then, one of our own, in the line of duty, shot me as I chased after a local national who was stealing something from one of the offices. I do not remember much, except for the burning in my right shoulder. I thought it was a pinched nerve. Then there was the pain in my left ankle, and then my feet seemed to appear in front of me. I was later told that I was shot by accident. After that, no one really wanted to talk to me, and I don't know why. However, I guess that is the price I had to pay for turning in the dumb ass for shooting me. At least he took me to the German hospital to get help. He even tried to cover it up and say I did this to myself. That was really funny. I don't make it a habit of going around shooting myself in the shoulder and then in the leg. Anyway, I will be here with you as I heal and get over my fears.

Dear Diary: 1988

I have grown depressed and lonely. I cannot stop thinking of the look on the enemies' faces as they stared back at me in anger, as both sides nearly killed each other, and the helicopter that stared me down as I was a sitting duck, frozen to my tiny, little jeep behind probably the best weapon we might have had, the M2 .50 caliber machine gun. The torture of the cold was unbearable. I think I made a few enemies here after telling the platoon sergeant that I had frostbite on my face. In my opinion, he just did not want to have to deal with the commander and all the paperwork that goes with it. However, in reality, there was very little paperwork and a doctor's visit, not an ass-chewing from the commander.

Dear Diary: 1988

I could not sleep. I keep waking up after seeing ghosts in my head. The same white faces of the past dead come to me as I sleep in this room. I hear the moans of the past. Why are they after me and why do they have to go through me?

Dear Diary: 1988

The chain of command has sent me off for an evaluation. They think I am crazy. I came back from the hospital just fine, and with a clean bill of health. It felt good to let out the past. I think I can move on now.

CHAPTER 6
Hobby or Lust

It was hard to believe that three years had already come and gone, and I found myself not wanting to leave. I had found a part of me here in Germany, as my love for the German culture grew by the minute, and I was having fun. During my three-year tour in Europe, I picked up singing while in a basement of the soldiers' recreation center. This was the point in my life where finding myself was going to be the most difficult task that God had ever given me. Singing allowed me to express myself. Starting off, I sounded like a little girl with a bad cold, but once I taught myself the ins and outs of singing, I hit the big time; well, it was the big time for me at the time, singing on weekends in the clubs around town, if I wasn't working. It didn't pay much, but I was doing what I loved to do, and you could say it was worth it, because I got all the girls. Those who were down there with me in the studios didn't care what I sounded like, because in my opinion, they were worse off then I was. I found myself doing gigs in some of the clubs in Mannheim, Germany, for starters, and then I moved on to small tours as we became better. There were times when I was asked to stand in for someone who had just quit or that was too sick to sing. That got me more money then I expected, and it gave me the opportunity to get the BMW that I had always wanted. This took me into a better phase of my life when I was starting to get good at singing. A Christian rock band asked me to audition with them, so I did. I played keyboard some and guitar, but my fetish was the drums. It was like a calling for me, and I had to play. On my days off, I would get into the hobby shop before anyone else and would play my heart out until everyone came in. The cool part is that I became good at it. Now I can sing, play guitar, keyboard, drums, and write music and lyrics. I was just a regular one-man tour, and I had finally found my outlet for stress. You ask if I had stress; well, let us just say it is not all being written here. I had my times that I wanted to wring a lot of people's necks, but I bit my tongue. Maybe if I would have spoken up, I might be higher ranking now and maybe not, but that is the chance one must take.

With that aside, I found myself through the eyes of a woman and my singing. There is a saying, "that with every good man, there is a good woman." Very true statement in my eyes, because that is all I would sit and think about sometimes when I am alone. When the peacefulness of quiet took me over as I sat alone, I would think of thousands of questions about women, like what they really wanted from a man, and they really wanted to be treated. What makes them tick inside? What type of love do they want from a man? What do they see in the type of man they really want, and do I have those qualities?

Well, the life of a singer did bring some girls, but the other band members got plenty of them, with their long hair and civilian rating. Being in the army, I had to keep a crew cut and military bearing to go with it. The nice part of not being married, like some of the other band members, was that I didn't have anyone to answer to when I got home at night. The bad part was that I didn't have anyone to go home to each day. It does have its ups and downs, but I was content with who I was.

Don't you just hate it after you say something like that, and then along comes this beautiful creature who just knocks your socks off? You know the one you cannot seem to take your eyes off of; the one who, when she looks over at you about a billion times, you can just tell it is the "one." Well it happened like this: one night I was singing in the sticks. That is what I called the basement of this studio. I left the window open, because the air conditioning wasn't working that day. I thought that no one would be able to hear me screeching aloud, but to my surprise, a shadow bent down to see inside the tiny room I was in, singing my heart out for the world to hear. I had headphones on, so I was not able to tell if the speakers were on. To my surprise, the music was playing "open-mic," so everyone could hear me singing. Not only was it loud but everyone was hearing me screech like an owl. I looked up, but to my surprise, the shadow was gone. A few minutes later, the shadow seemed to have appeared at the studio door. I went to answer the door during one of the breaks, and to my surprise, a stunning girl stood there. She had long, brown hair that reached her butt. Her skin was soft, pale, and very well taken care of, and she had just a touch of makeup on. She had on a tight dress shirt that cropped at the shoulders and rounded the neckline; with a matching blue-jean miniskirt and white, high-heel pumps. To go with those pumps were the most unbelievably sexy legs that a man could dream of; you know, the type that look like they have pantyhose on, but don't; the ones that are so well taken care of that you know they are soft. Hers shined when the light hit them, and she didn't have on pantyhose. She was just stopping in to see where the music was coming from, and she asked if she could come in to sit in on the practice. I let her in, and she took her place on the near side of the room next to the recording microphone that I was sitting next to. I told her I was just finishing up for the night and was going to go get something to eat. She was just going over to the Pizza Palace across the quad when she heard the music and stopped to see where it was coming from.

Obeying my stomach first, I walked with this very hot mommy to the Pizza Palace to get something to eat. We talked more as we devoured the pizza in front of us. It was obvious that she was trying to keep that sexy figure, because she only ate one piece of pizza. After small talk, I found out that her name was Dawn. It was such a nice name that fit her well. The entire time I was eating the pizza, Dawn would stare at me and smile. It was like a devious look in her eyes that saw something she wanted. I just couldn't believe that it was me that she wanted until she asked me to go for a walk. She didn't want to go home, and she wanted to get to know me more. With that said, I also wanted to get to know her, and in more ways then one; but it wasn't the time for that right now. We made our way out to a lake, where we sat on the edge of the lake and watched the night lights dance off the water. Dawn was a little cold, and she seemed comfortable with me as she snuggled between my legs, and I wrapped my arms around her to keep her warm. The fact of the matter is that she was keeping me warm. We talked for hours, until the cold took over, and we made our way to my barracks room. Dawn called her mother and told her where she was going to be staying for the night, and that she was okay. Her mother knew that she could take care of herself, so we sat up talking and eating German Danishes the rest of the night, until we fell asleep. The next morning, I quickly got up and quietly made some coffee as I watched her sleep. She looked so cute there on the bed, all cuddled up to my pillow.

So you ask if I was a good boy; well, in this case, yes, because she was only sixteen at the time. In Germany and in most places, someone of her caliber can be given permission to marry at that age, but it just wasn't right for me at that moment. Dawn started to move with that unbelievably sexy stretch. I think girls practice that in school or something. Weeks would be spent getting to know each other.

It is really funny how lights in a club can play a trick on you when you have been drinking. While singing at the Taylor Barracks Club in Mannheim, Germany, I thought that I had landed the girl of my dreams. Boy was I wrong. At least I didn't think so at the time. She looked like a high-school knockout in my eyes, and something inside told me to stay clear. Being that the passion raged inside me and I had this insight inside my tiny head that I had to conquer her. We locked eyes, and those beautiful hazel eyes put me in a trance. She played me like a cheap guitar as she moved her position so that her legs would show more and fluffing her hair as if to send a mating call like birds during the mating season. The lights from the stage made me a star that night, yet I knew that she would not be leaving with me that night. It would have to be while I was on duty as a military policeman that I'd run into her again, in the PX parking lot, with her mom. Call it coincidence that I had to receive a call from dispatch to assist a downed motorist there. I was to be her knight in shining armor, as the vehicle they were driving broke down. Their car battery started a fire in the engine compartment and was spreading into the rest of the car. Grabbing the fire extinguishers from the patrol car, I quickly extinguished the flames and disconnected the battery that was causing the problem. I turned around, only to see Dawn staring at me once again. Not thinking, I had to yell to get her and her family to a safe distance in the event that the vehicle exploded or something. Within minutes, the fire department came and took the battery out of the vehicle and explained the problem to Dawn's mother. Without skipping a beat, she went into the PX, purchased another one, and attempted to replace it. As I helped replace the battery, it was then that we both remembered we had run into each other before. It was when I had just joined into the army and was home on leave in Tucson, Arizona, at the Park Mall. At the time, they were also living in Tucson, just up the street from me. Dawn's mother was assigned as a schoolteacher in Germany. As fate had it for us, we started to hit it off really well as she explained how she just got out of a really bad relationship with another soldier. I finished putting the battery in their raggedy old Volvo station wagon. Dawn's mother seemed really nice, and she took a liking to me, as Dawn explained that we actually lived in the same town, and how we actually knew each other from Tucson. Her mother just couldn't say enough as she invited me out for dinner with them that night. It was a small gesture for fixing her vehicle, as I started up the Volvo and a smile came upon all of their faces. I was not allowed to accept the invitation, and I didn't want to be rude about it, so I waited until Dawn begged me to accept the invitation. Gladly accepting, Dawns face lit up so bright, you could have bottled the glow up and lit half of Mannheim, Germany with it. The rest of the day tortured me as the thought of Dawn danced in my head.

Dear Diary: 1988

Today is a bad day for me. I do not remember much, and I only know what was told to me. I had just woken up from a bad accident after I was shot twice by one of our very own; once in the right shoulder and the other in the left ankle. I do know that it hurts like hell, being shot by a .45-caliber pistol even if it was an accident. The nurse is telling me that I have to go to sleep, so I had better go for now. Damn, she is hot in that white see-through dress. I know, shame on me, but I am right.

Dawn would give up her time with most of her friends to spend time with me down in the studio. I would take time to spend with her by going to castles and walking in the forests on Volks Marches. Still, something inside would test me, and I would come to regret this passion I had for one woman. We had plenty of time getting to know each other, and it was beautiful. I finally found someone who could connect with me and understand me. She was young, as was I, and we didn't want to be rushed into anything. Months were spent getting to know her family, until her mother asked me to move in with them off the base, where Dawn and I could be together more.

I slowed down on the time spent on tours to crystal and chocolate factories and turned to spending more time in the studio to brush up on my singing. I was working on a piece as I sat at the drums one day in the studio, and an amateur rock group member, kind of like myself, came into the studio and took the room two doors from me. The band had set up and tested their equipment as I played on. One of the members came to the door where I was and peered through the small, Plexiglas window and watched me play my piece. I never noticed him until after I finished recording the vocal set. He must have liked it, because the others showed up at the door and wanted to hear my set, so I obliged them and sang my heart out at the microphone. Once the set was finished, I was asked to stand in as a backup singer as the band played the music of Def Leppard. I joined in the singing, as the lead singer, Steve, stepped out of the picture and sat down and watched as I tore up the room. I thought I had many spectators, but this group had many groupies that they must have brought with them. I was feeling very much at home in the small room that barely could fit the band's equipment and a few chairs. During a break, Steve asked if I would show off a bit for the groupies and sing with them. I was already pretty shy and self-conscious about my voice, but I did it anyway. The rewards were stunning. It seemed to come naturally to me being able to sing and be in front of people. I felt a calming sensation inside as the words to the songs just came out like rings of shining gold. I had found my outlet for the world's bullshit that just seemed to pile itself on to my plate every time I come to the serving line. When I sang, all that went away, and I loved life. Being a member of the military, I really did not seem to have a lot of time, but to me it was enough to do the things that I wanted to do. I got to see a great deal of Europe, meet a lot of people, and find myself. I had the chance to blossom and become someone; someone that Dad could be proud of.

The band played a few more songs and then took a break, which was my cue to exit the place and get back to the barracks to get a change of clothes before I went over to Dawn's house, not knowing that I would be greeted by her at the barracks door. You know, this girl was amazing in so many ways. She had this startling walk as she walked with such ladylike grace. I loved watching her walk away. She had a swing that would take you to the stars. Many times when we dated, I felt as if I was compelled to walk her home, so we took the long route, getting to know each other. It seemed to be enough time to ask her the important questions. "Hello. Can I ask you a question? Oh, by the way, I am Thomas." I sounded as if I was from a Tarzan movie: "Me Tarzan, you Jane." She turned me all to mush as she stopped to sit on the edge of a rock at the nearby hangout; the lake, where we always went. She seemed to want to talk to me when she answered back with, "I am Dawn." She played with every emotion in my body as she straightened her legs out and put her hands between her legs, which in turn pushed her breasts together, and with a smile, she pleasantly waited for my next comment. I was speechless as she stared at me with the most powerful hazel eyes.

I just couldn't resist asking her the ultimate question that gets most men turned down right away; the one that is the killer of most startup relationships. Nevertheless, it is a chance you have to take. "So are you seeing anyone?" I asked.

I felt like an ass right away for asking, and I was sure that she was going to be turned off, but I was wrong.

"I am, but he can wait," she replied with a settled and confident voice. It was as if the fantasy in her just took her and handed her to me. It must have been a bad relationship, and Dawn must really like me at this point to want me to move in and hang out a lot. So where was Romeo; the one who called himself her boyfriend? With that over, it was obvious that she liked me from this point on. We talked for hours and got to know each other. In getting to know each other, it started to appear as though we were from the same city and states within the United States, and it was as if we had known each other for the longest time. As dusk rolled in and Dawn began to get cold, it seemed like the right time to cuddle with each other.

"Are you cold?" I asked, knowing damned well that she was. "Do you want to go?"

To my surprise, she didn't skip a beat. "No. We can stay out for a little longer. Besides it is nice out here, and I like being with you." We walked along Vogelstein Lake holding each other's hand, and Dawn seemed to be clinging to me as we watched the moonlight glitter and dance off of the lake water. I couldn't help but notice that she was holding onto my arm and hand pretty tightly as we walked. It seemed as though she didn't want any of this to end. We stopped at a bridge that overlooked the lake and saw a team of white geese swimming nearby. Dawn turned and faced me, and wrapping her arms around my waist and hugging me, she put her head on my chest. "You feel so good, you know." And, as any man would, I began to get a wood from the feel of her body next to mine. It was as if she knew how to make me reach the manhood stage. It was not something that I was really good at by this point in my life. She was a real woman, and she was about to become my teacher in sex education. Germany sure does teach you things about yourself and life, and Dawn looked up at me, expecting a kiss or something. It was that time that I had been waiting for all day it seemed. I took a chance of risking humiliation by kissing her. It was the most sensual kiss that I have ever had from any woman. There, on the bridge, for the world to see, we made out like two horny rabbits. Never did I know that I would be having sex on a bridge in public for the world to see. Any passerby could be watching or even report us to the police, but that wasn't the case. It was as if none of that even mattered as Dawn and I expressed our gratitude to each other though sex. She felt like no other girl I had ever been with. In this case, she was a woman, and I was becoming a man inside. She showed me things that made me see the light and realize the truth of a thousand women's true fantasies. And now I saw the truth behind the phrase:

"Behind every good man is a good woman."

Or is there?

It wasn't long before I was wrestled into the decision of getting out of the army. Dawn and I grew into a relationship of inseparable love, or so it seemed. Spending just about every minute together didn't seem to blemish our hearts before God, and marking the day as we planned an elaborate white wedding at the officers' club. It was incredible for a wedding by most standards. Dawn's father, being the rich man he was, wanted the very best for his little girl, so he had all the fixings. Sadly, he never showed his face at the wedding of his daughter. Any self-righteous father would be there for his daughter, to see her standing, reciting the wedding vows, and growing up for the entire world to see. I nearly passed out from all the stress of a wedding and the sight of Dawn's beauty. It is a typical role of the groom to forget his wedding vows and pass out while trying to say them, but don't get me wrong ladies and gentlemen. All of this does come with a painful price, one that I did not expect in the not-too-distant future. With the formalities out of the way, let the party begin. Just about every guest at the wedding brought crystal, as a gift to the bride; you know, the Post Exchange kind, the cheap way to get out of buying a present because, they couldn't think of a good one to bring at the last minute. Some had the sense to give baby clothes, but something told me that we were not going to be having children. Call it what you want, but I had a gut feeling that we were not going to be having children at all. I prayed, like any husband did, to be able to give the world to your new bride, yet that little something deep inside kept telling me that something was not right. It was the kind of feeling you get when you just know that getting married was a huge mistake. I silently played it off throughout the year as Dawn and I vacationed around Germany like newly-weds, conquering the castles of Heidelberg and Mannheim and spending time at the Christmas Marts. The hard part for me was when I had to send Dawn to live with my father in Arizona as I out processed from the active army. It didn't seem like a bad thing. The phone bill said something worse. Running up a fifteen-hundred –dollar-a-month phone bill over love was getting a little ridiculous. Dawn never really cared for the military, yet she toyed with its people just for fun, and I happened to be one of those toys to her. Only the selected elite would win her heart over, and I had the privilege to taste the ripened fruit of this slab of meat. I think it was just a way out for her that we got married and she was sent home to America. The reality of it all is that I was whipped like any other young whippersnapper out there. Still, to this day, I ask myself why I did it. Was it all for the girl and pride, or the fact that I was just plan dumb and horny? Did I think that I could make a difference in this girl's life after all that she had been through? That was not likely, but there was the chance that it could happen. The white wedding was huge. Friends from far and near came to see the marriage from the fairy tale books. Yes, it was that kind of wedding. I felt really out of place and not welcome at my own wedding. Most of the friends were there for Dawn and her side of the family. Trying to get them to see the bride and groom as "lovebirds" was just not going to happen. It was here that I would recognize that I was becoming superstitious. Have you ever heard the saying, "Have a big wedding, the marriage doesn't last; have a small wedding, the marriage lasts forever"? Well you will come to know this, so trust me on that one.

CHAPTER 7

Total Devastation

I thought that being married would have a profound impact on my life as a man, but I had come to know women in a different way since my childhood days. Let it be known that the saying, "Beauty is in the eyes of the beholder" is, in fact, true. I thought for years that it would be so easy to have a beautiful woman by your side and all would be good. Boy, was I wrong. I found that it was nothing but trouble. Dawn, my first wife, pampered as she was, had it all; at least what I could give her. She was about as high maintenance as you can get. Dear old Daddy made sure of that as she grew up. Of course, how can you turn down your own little girl. She learned, all too early in life, that all she had to do was just bat her eyebrows and she got everything she wanted. Then there is the infamous smile and the torturous body that did the rest. Nevertheless, you know those smiles, and they played on this man's mind. To me, at my age, a smile was just a sign of something else at play. Since the days of innocence, men have evolved into another form of human figure as "women's right's activists," stepped in and demanded more positions at the top. Well, fine with me. Hell, if you ask me, I would gladly stay at home and take care of the kids or clean the house.

Ha, ha, ha.

Now that would be a challenge, because I already know how to do that. There was one good thing that came out of having a stepmother. She taught my brother and I to do just about anything on our own. And those things that we didn't know, we learned on our own through trial and error. I don't think they would like the way I did things, but at least it would get done. And yes, it is a fact that I live a clean life. When I was a bachelor, I had a very clean house. I had to invite a woman over to get it all messy sometimes, but you know how it is. They bitch all the time about how things are too clean, yet the simple fact of the matter is, woman, by nature, are dirtier than men.

As I sent Dawn home to live at my father's house for a short while as I left the military life behind and returned home from Germany, a very strange feeling came over me as I entered United States airspace. I couldn't put a finger on it, but it wasn't good for me. It was as if my world would be turned upside down some time in the future, as if the future had something to tell me, but couldn't. The homecoming wasn't all bells and whistles, as some would have thought. The hate from civilians was the same as that for the Vietnam veterans. I guess the protectors of the world don't need a thank you, or even a smile, but that is the downfall of the cold-war era.

I spent a little time with my new bride before reporting to my reserve unit in Arizona as a Bradley mechanic. I attended art school during the day and worked weekends for my father as an electrician's helper, to keep gas in the truck. My reserve unit was cool to me, because I was the only military policeman in the bunch. Every drill, "the unit speeders" would come and see me, begging me to try to get them out of their speeding tickets. The sheriff was fair, but I was not able to save the fish from the flame. It's funny how, at every drill, the unit would have a huge barbeque during the last day of the drill, because the cooks didn't want to cook anything in the clean kitchen for the troops. Just about everyone had a grill of some sort, and they would bring their own steaks or chicken, and we all sat and grilled steaks and chicken while drinking beer and playing ball. It was our way of bonding with one another. It was what some would say was the biggest, and baddest, cook-off in the state of Arizona. There were so many cooks, and so little time to eat all the food brought. I don't blame them for doing that, because it was more fun, and it tasted better anyway. Military food has guidelines that have to be followed. There were no guidelines to grilling, except one: don‘t burn the steaks. I didn't really care, I just wanted the food that was cooked on the damn thing. Nevertheless, what can you say for a bunch of armor grunts? They know how to have a good time and stick together. My time spent in that armor unit, was probably the best I have had in the army. The reserves was a different world from active duty in the ways of teamwork. The unit had its issues, but no one really seemed to care. Everyone came together for one another during each drill.

The commander really didn't know me, but how can you expect to know everyone with the amount of soldiers he had to deal with? I was the outcast, if you will; the one oddball that fit in nicely and kept his mouth shut. But what can I say; I never really liked officers to begin with. When it came time to fix things, that is where I had the most impact. I scored very high on my ASVAB test in the technical section, so that makes a difference; yet, I scored really high in all subjects. I guess you can say that my "I.Q." was up there, but I never really cared.

Like any unit you go to, there were your typical whiners and complainers, as well as those who just didn't want to do anything, but like I said, that is everywhere you go in the military. Don't let the buffer of the "esprit de corps" fool you, we all have our times in the military. I can say one thing about those that I have run into over the years of service; you know, the ones who say: "I'm not going to do anything today;" or, "You want what and when?"; Or even better, "Those insecure, self-centered kiss-asses."

They are the ones who just scrape by, doing the bare minimum to get to the top so they can do nothing all day, anyway. They are the ones who you meet up with later in life and you have to make the choices for them, because they took the easy road. There is one thing I can say for myself as a man: "I am an honest man to myself."

Besides, if I don't, then who will be? And being my typical self, I didn't find ways to get out of things. I found new ways to get into things. This would be my concept of learning over the years. With all that I now know and all that I have done over the years, I can thank myself for not giving in or taking the easy road. I now have the skills to do that which needs to be done. I am not saying I know it all, but I can say I know a lot, because I have done it myself.

I guess this is the part when someone once said, "Ask not what your country can do for you, but what you can do for your country."

I did just that. I took the bull by the horns and rode that sumbitch 'til it croaked.

I never stopped to see the rosy side of life. I got into the thick of it all while the rest stood on the sidelines and did nothing but socialize. Think of it as a good book. When you start reading it, you know you are going to go to places that thousands have traveled before you, either in person, or through knowledge; yet the outcome for some was grim, and others had the life of luxury. I look at it as my life of "everything possible." I still have a hard time believing in fairness towards some when it comes to learning something in this life, but one thing I can say is that I have been taught.

I spent a good two years in the reserves before Dawn and I moved up to Phoenix, Arizona, where we would try to make a living on our own. Dad and Cheryl would come up from time to time to make sure we had food, and that everything was okay. Like any parent, they would take you grocery shopping and fill the bare cabinets. This was the life of college students. We were roughing it through the time that was spent in classes or the studying late at night. We both attended College at the DeVry Institute of Technology in Phoenix. Dawn took classes for "business organizational management" and I was an "electronic engineering technologist." They were two very good majors, but for me, it was all starting to slip as I sat back and watched Dawn melt away from me.

Dear Dairy: 1989

Dawn does not seem to want to be with me anymore. She has let herself go and has gained a great deal of weight again. She is starting to blame her weight and unhappiness on me, now. I suspect that there is another reason, but I cannot prove it at this point. She goes to her friends to study an awful lot. I have a suspicion, but I think she might be pregnant. Just a few weeks ago, she wanted me to take her to the doctors, but she did not want to show me any of the paperwork, nor did she want me to go with her. I think she is going in for an abortion.

It was as if I were out of her league as she focused on her career. I was just moving along to the beat with her, but she never really paid much attention to me, and we started to grow further and further apart. From time to time, she would blame her massive weight gain on me, because she was unhappy, but that did not mean anything to me. I was in love with her, and that mattered most to me. Yet all she had to do was pay more attention to me; instead she paid more mind, body and her study partner that took the studying too far. I had a funny feeling that something was going on, but I just could not put my finger on it. The flashbacks from the plane ride home from Germany kept flashing in my head over and over again. It was as if I knew what I would find to be true. Getting on my motorcycle, I drove to the apartments where she studied at, only to find that she and her so-called study partner were not studying the literature within the books at all. It was more like the teachings of lust. I sat staring into the bottom-floor apartment window as they romped on the bed. She seemed so happy being with him. It wasn't like they tried to hide anything from anyone that passed. They were in a bottom-floor apartment with the bedroom-window blinds wide open for all to see. It was obvious that she wanted me to find her like this. I returned home and tried to get back to my studies as she calmly walked into our studio apartment. She immediately went to the bathroom and showered before even kissing her husband who she had so willingly cheated on. I thought, for the time we were together, that it was just me, yet I found that my friends who nurtured me through this troubling time kept reassuring me that it was not me. Larry was a good friend, and he always had a way of showing me that life is what you make it, not what is in it. He eased my pain as I left the apartment and drove to the one topless bar that he always liked to go to. Larry had the hots for the ladies. I got a kick out of watching him piss his hard-earned cash away on girls he thought he would get into bed. I never did find out if he did or not.

Dear Diary: 1989-1990

Dawn has been involved with another, and I am sure of it now. I just saw her sleeping with another man when she said they were just study partners. She does not want to come home with me now, so I left her there at the apartment with him, knowing what has just happened. With this no longer a secret, and the fact that I confirmed she did have an abortion, I do not want to be with her anymore, either, yet I still love her and want to try to make this work out.

Dear Dairy: 1990

We moved into a new apartment last week. We also had to get a few roommates to help with the rent. This was my way of getting away from her more, as I know she is cheating on me more and more when I am gone with Larry.

Dear Diary: June 1990

The military has just called me up for active duty. I am to report in a few days to go over to the Persian Gulf. Things have been heating up pretty quickly over there. It is amazing how the reign of hate can cross the world so quickly. Dawn doesn't like the fact that I will be going, but she does not seem to be too heartbroken over it, either. Just a hint guys and gals, this is the part when you know they are cheating: too many tell-tell signs. Hell, I would not be surprised if Larry even had sex with her, too. That guy tried so many times to get into her pants, that I was even learning things from him.

At this point, I needed the one thing that only made sense to me. The military life was the only true love that I had and understood, so without hesitation, I ran off to see the retention office for the army. They didn't have much in the field that I had worked in the past, but they did have an opening for an EOD specialist in the national guard; that is "explosives, ordinance, and disposal," for those that don't understand military acronyms. I spent the next three years of my life in the national guard, trying to make sense of what I had done wrong, but never did. During my time in the guard, I excelled past those who did this for a living. I attended college for the time that I had left in the day, but it just wasn't enough to get me over the pain of Dawn cheating on me. As we grew more and more apart, I started to search for something more in my life, and she saw right through this. Dawn started to get closer to me as I began to pull away from her. She knew something was wrong, and that it was not good for her. I spent more time outdoors and away from the house than I did with her before. One reason for this was the fact that we were hurting for money, and we were pulling apart, so why not start looking for a roommate. We discussed the plans for a roommate, then offered it to Larry. He moved in with us just as he snared a mate. Becky, in my opinion was not right for him, but this was the one person he had chosen to be with, so I let him be. The sharing of food and rent helped a great deal as I planned my next move. I went to and from drills with the national guard and spent a good majority of my time in the lab at the school. This was my excuse to see the one blossom that I had been eyeballing for over a month now. She was so; well, let me say this: she was everything Dawn was not.

Dear Diary: 1991

Dawn #1, and I have pretty much called it quits. I came home from the Gulf War and found a new itch in life. My time spent there was utterly the worst time of my military career. I have never seen death as I saw it there. I just cannot get it out of my head. The problems started to mount up as Dawn #1, and I separated, yet I still had the Gulf War in my head. Returning to school was not something I wanted to do, so I stalled out for a while. Dawn #1, was just finishing her time there and trying so hard to find me after I left the apartment. The funny part is that she never even knew that I was only a few blocks from her and saw her every-painful day. However, my savior came in the form of an angel. She was incredible; everything Dawn #1, was not and she wanted me for sure. As Dawn #1, filed divorce papers, I did my homework. I can't wait to see this young thing again. I will be taking her out on a date tonight, and then I hope to bring her back to the apartment.

The entire five foot-one, ninety-eight-pound package just turned me on. She had the spice that I needed in my life. Whenever I saw her, I got chills, as I did when I was in elementary school; you know, guys, that feeling you had when you saw the one true love of your life, or so you thought and that is what really mattered then. I wore mirrored sunglasses all the time so I could check her out without her seeing where I was looking. There was one time when I was walking down the hall and I tripped over someone's book bag, because I wasn't watching where I was going. That was the effect she had over me. Everything about her made me snap to attention. I wasn't even sure that she noticed me at all, but I wanted her in a bad way. I wished, from time to time, that I could switch Dawn #1, for Dawn #2, and that she and I would go home together and just cuddle on the couch and pretend that nothing was wrong with our life together. Then reality would slap me in the face and wake me up as the instructor passed by rattling his key for the world to hear, and would I have to remember that I was married and had to go home to the one I know has cheated with the same guy that I went to lab with. Nevertheless, in reality, it just did not matter anymore as I looked into Dawn's #2, eyes and saw the smile on her face. She had the medicine that was the cure for every ounce of pain that I had at the time.

My big chance came as we sat in computer lab and the instructor asked us all to pair up. I had to think quickly on my feet, and I turned to see her sitting behind me. I asked her if she wanted to be my partner without hesitation, and she quickly replied, without missing a beat "sure." I remember the denim skirt she wore that day, with the tight sleeveless top. She sat with her legs crossed and upright ever so perfect. I couldn't take my eyes off how beautiful she looked. To top off the rest, she had the most upstanding legs I had ever seen. As she spoke, it was as if the world around us had stopped, and for a moment, nothing mattered. I just couldn't let this go at all. She asked if I was married, and I replied that I was on a piece of paper, but that I was going through a divorce. She responded back, but the answer didn't register in my head. I quickly wrote on the paper, "I would if I could anyway."

It was as if time had stopped there and then for us as she looked deep into my eyes.

"Can I give you a ride home or something?"

She replied, "Yes," and we gathered our things and left the lab, not knowing that this would be a day to remember forever. She lived pretty far outside of city limits, but I didn't mind. I felt at home with her, as she had her arms wrapped around my waist while we rode through town. I didn't even care that I was supposed to meet my wife and take her home. I wanted to be with this girl forever. While I was dropping her off at her mailbox, she pulled me to her, and she kissed me for the first time. It was at that moment that I knew she was the one. It was as if nothing in the world mattered anymore. My life changed at that time and place as the electricity built up within her and me. I had found my soulmate, and she was everything I had expected and more. I think my actual spouse knew that it was ending, and she rather abruptly packed for an invitation to California to stay with her girlfriend for a week. This was my time to move in on the kill zone and take total advantage of what I wanted more in this world. With the enemy gone "Dawn #1." Dawn #2, and I spent the week walking out on the town as if we were alive. Then we went home to the apartment and held each other like nothing else mattered in this world. Being with her took away the pain of the rest of the world and the worries melted away. It wasn't long after this that she and I engaged in activities that brought our first son into this desperate world. It would then be a year or so when we would marry and move into a new life; just the three of us. I was a proud father and husband. This is what I had hoped for, for the longest time, and that dream had come true finally. Something Dawn #1, never wanted at all. Little did she know that I knew more about what she was doing behind my back, and then some. I even knew about the child that we had, but she gave up to the gods for nothing but the memory of the child that could have been. Dawn had me pictured as an ignorant person, but as I came up through the ranks I learned from the mistakes of the others around me. My upbringing taught me a few things as well.

Dear Diary: 1991

Dawn #1, is gone, and I now have a new and improved Dawn. She is everything that Dawn #1 was not, and more. She had to go to a graduation party, and I am fearful that she will not be coming back to me, so I made plans to see her next week. I can hardly wait for her to come over. It is driving me nuts, so I think I will go out to the Jacuzzi for a soak.

CHAPTER 8

From One Land to Another

Years seemed to pass quickly as I found myself divorced from the first Dawn and married to the new and improved Dawn; my soulmate, if you will. I guess I am a sucker for the name Dawn. The humor of this whole thing is that I would never get into trouble in bed if I were sleeping around with another Dawn, and called out her name by accident. Not that I would sleep with another at this point, and I did not have any reason to sleep around.

As things progressed, so did the love for this woman. She was everything that my ex-wife was not. This one wanted to be next to me all the time. There were times I had to take time away from her to be with myself. I was smothered in love and passion as if no other woman has even loved me before; not that I was a Casanova or anything, but Dawn just had me wrapped up around her finger and she didn't even know it at this point.

While I was trying to find time for a new family, college, and warding off the pain of a divorce, the military came calling once again. To help you understand why I got out the first time, Dawn, my first wife, didn't like the military, just the Joes; in this case, me. She did not want to live the life of an army wife, so being the young man I was, I got out of the army and went into the reserves. I just didn't feel right about letting it all go for a woman. In this case, I was letting go of more than I had realized, as things heated up around the world and in my life. I was divorced one day, sent off to the fight in the Gulf war, Desert Shield and Desert Storm, and then I came home to be remarried all over again. It's funny how things changed so fast as I went through a time warp as fast as I did. Nevertheless my head was thrown a little out of whack from the Gulf War as well. For starters, real war in the past was kids stuff to the urban and guerilla warfare being fought today. Weapons that are more special are being used, along with chemicals. It was not something, I intended on seeing or coming into contact with, but as a former cold-war veteran, I can tell you that it is still around and in the enemy's hands. The sad part was seeing all the destruction and death in plain view. The media had nothing on soldiers as far as I could see it. They had it easy, compared to the rest. Going out on patrol at night was like going out during the day with all the oil wells burning. Cars, trucks, tanks, and other various types of vehicles were along the side of the road, with human remains still hanging out of the vehicles; either burned to a crisp or just plain dead. The smell reminded me a bit of the time I was a kid in Marana, Arizona, where I grew up on a ranch and remember smelling the cattle's skin as it was burned from the branding. It is the sweet smell you never forget. It is not the same as barbequing in the backyard, either. This type of smell makes you remember the death. Some even stared you down as you passed by them in their state of death. They eyes told their legacy, but how gut wrenching it is to have it told in that way.

The wretched, thick, black smoke from the fires choked you almost to death. A clean uniform was worn most everyday, but after a while you just stop caring about going out in clean clothes, only to come back from patrol in black, soot-filled clothes. The oil from the fields was now in my lungs and clothes, as well as the rest of my body and personal things. I don't think there was a clean item I had.

The longer we were there in this horrible combat situation and the more missions we went on, the more active everything became. The Nat's, A-10 Thunderbolts, flew around the sky, as if they were in heat, killing almost anything; they saw fit to include the friendly side, too. There was not a lot of fratricide, but there was enough t` remember. Taking the main city was a chore. We sat for days, waiting for the main forces to rush in as we held the perimeter and waiting on the enemy to be flushed out somewhere. Small amounts of firefights turned into an all out gun battles as a wall of lead stood up in front of the enemy. I guess they thought we were playing "Cowboys and Indians," because after the first few gun battles, I had lost all interest in the killing of any human. The moment when you are looking down the sights of a rifle and you have to choose between your life and his, you tend to choose his life over yours. The dirt trench I laid in was not deep enough when the bullets began to whiz past my head. However, I somehow overcame the fear of death when I pulled the trigger and saw him fall. He went out of this world with honor, but for the wrong cause. Even so, he was in a better place now. I still live with the thought of his death. Nightmares torture me almost every day, still; flashbacks of the dead, burned bodies and total devastation of entire cities; animals starving to death as you pass by, along with refugees that line the roadside trying to get out of the battle-torn areas. The rationale that came over me then, was that I meant nothing to them. We, as a nation, had destroyed the only life these people ever had, and now they had nothing. I felt lower than the bugs that crawled on the ground. Nothing could prepare me for what was about to happen next.

Dear Diary: 1992

Sorry I have not written in so long. I have good news. I have a son and his name is Matheuw. It just happened one night after a barbeque that I had at the apartment. Dawn came over and stayed the night. It was a big change from the old Dawn. I felt very much at home when she came in the door. Here is how it all happened. We made plans to spend the day together, but never thought about having friends over for a barbeque. Therefore, we went to the town fair and walked around. Then we sat eating as the sun went down. The light hit her eyes just right and thawed my cold and bitter heart. I felt so comfortable with Dawn. She cuddled next to me the entire time we were together, as if we were inseparable, and that is what I was counting on. Back at the apartment, our friends kept pulling us apart, and of course, the Joes tried to intercept her, but she would just keep coming back to me. It was funny how it all worked out in the end. We could no longer stand it, and we kicked everyone out at about eleven o'clock. I thought she wanted me to take her home, but instead she asked if I wanted to cuddle on the couch and watch a movie. The next thing I knew, we were waking up in the bed and thinking that we were late for work. Good thing it was the weekend, so we just got up and went out to have brunch. Before we knew it, Matheuw was starting to show, and things really took on a new meaning for me. This is what I had been waiting for all my life; something that my now-ex-wife refused to cherish: the joy of life. Oh, well, that is her loss. I have been given the gift of life through this woman now before me.

Dear Diary: 1993

Dawn #2 and I have moved back to Tucson with my father. Dawn and I are making plans to get married in May, and I need to get the hell away from Dawn #1. She has been a real thorn in my side since she and I divorced. I lost a great deal in the divorce, and she made out like the fat rat that she is. The funny thing is that she went back to her old job, and when I stopped in, she did not even know how to take a compliment. What a bitch.

Dear Diary: May 7, 1994

Today is a glorious day for Dawn and me. We are to be married before I reenter active duty for the third time. I was hoping for this, because I wanted to be back in the military anyway; back where I understand the people better and the way of life that it is. It is a good life, if you can handle being away from home all the time. Dawn has never been a military wife before, so this should prove to be a challenge for me, as it will be for her. We are slotted to go back overseas to Germany next month. I think she will like it, because she has never been out of the country before.

My God, she is beautiful in her wedding dress. We had a small wedding. It was nothing like the first one. My first marriage that turned a flop cost thousands and lasted only a few years. I thought I would turn the time back and take it one-step further. I sold the old wedding band and we decided on a set that only cost $35 total. They were plain gold bands, and it was enough for the Justice of the Peace. As we stood in line for the "J.P.," other couples were smiling at us as we kissed, like newlyweds. Of course, we were the youngest ones there. After the court wedding, we had to rush to the chapel to get married by the pastor. It was a very small wedding, with just family and friends, not an extravagance like before. I think the total cost of the wedding was $172 for everything, unlike the $8234 it cost for me to get married the first time. Never the less, I felt a change within as we said our vows.

With my rebellious attitude towards others at this point in my career and life, nurtured by the hate that was unleashed on my family and me, during our stay in Germany for the second time, I gained the respect that I now hold true. This newfound love for life opened up inside of me and was showing me the world. It offered hope that I would be loved forever, and all that had happened at this point didn't matter now.

I think my ex-wife called Germany and told them that we were coming here, because ever since I joined the military again, I had not had any luck with my tour of duty in Germany. She had to know someone over here. I was constantly being called for duty or given extra duties that other soldiers didn't have, because they had a hand up in the platoon._During my stay in Germany the second time, I would, however find the groove that no one else could detect. This would be the turning point for my newfound life and me.

As the chain of command struggled to have me chaptered out of the army for frivolous things, they never thought that one day someone like me would come along and change their little reign of terror on the weak and the unknowing. I gained the knowledge of thousands in the short time I was there and fought back. I turned their false accusations into fuel for me to fight, using the very system they used against my family and me. Moreover, all along the way, I educated myself with the laws of the land. As I readied myself for the first wave of deployment to Bosnia, Dawn was pregnant with our second son. With her not knowing how to survive on her own, I was left behind with her in the rear detachment, but not before the chain of command would play cat and mouse with me and have me going one hour, then staying the next. We fought with the chain of command for months, until I got tired of it one day and almost killed a man over honor.

It all started one day in an office meeting as I entered the unit for the first time. My first mistake was not being a sports fan; at least that was what my take on this issue was. My grudge held steadfast within me as my newest chain of command belittled me during my greeting, because I was not a sports fan. Gambling on sports was their pastime, and they didn't want anyone to jeopardize that. I would come to know "fantasy football" as the most hateful phrase in my ears. I still think it might be the way I reacted to the conversation as I talked with the squad leader and the platoon leader. I just plain came out and said, "I don't do sports. Well I do, but only gymnastics."

After the platoon office cooled off, it was explained to me that I needed to keep my mouth shut about the gambling that went on there. I did not know how to take that, but it probably was for the better that I kept my mouth shut.

I performed very well in the field because I had prior military experience. It would not be long before the unit would be activated for a tour in Bosnia. I can tell you that this was not expected, and I truly was not ready for this, as I was new to the unit and I had a new wife and son; but I made the best of a bad thing. I trained for the deployment and did what was needed of me to prepare, but one thing set me apart from the rest, and I would have to stay back. This did not sit right in the eyes of the unit or the chain of command. The turning point for my family and I was when the platoon sergeant, his wife, and the platoon leader came to my home and sat down with my spouse. I had been bedridden and out cold from the flu, so I was not able to get the blunt of the stick that was thrown hard at my wife.

Dear Diary: June 1994
The day is coming for a reckoning. I've dreamt of great amounts of hostilities and confrontations. The mass of many will be at my feet as I stamp out the flames of hate that have crossed into my path. There will be no end for years to come, as I struggle with the hate of the many. I will travel many worlds, and soon it will come that I will settle with my own ways as a commoner.

The next morning, Dawn sat over me, crying, as I woke up to her tears hitting my face. Seeing Dawn cry was not a good sign, and she tried to explain what had happened.

"That asshole platoon sergeant! I can't believe he called me useless!"

"What? Wait, start over from the beginning."

"Well, we were all sitting in the living room, and the platoon sergeant's wife explained to me the deployment. Then the platoon sergeant just looked at me and said that I was useless as an army wife, because I couldn't do anything on my own."

"What? He said that to you in my home?"

"Yes, and then his bitch of a wife told him it was time to go."

At about this point, I was burning inside, and I wanted some answers, but it couldn't just stop there.

"He also wanted me to give you a message. He said that if you don't get your shit ready for this deployment, then he will chapter you out of his freakin' army."

"Oh, really! He said that?"

"Yes."

"Okay then. I will take care of this myself, right now."

I pushed my way out of bed and got dressed for work, not knowing what would happen at this point, and knowing that it really didn't matter at this point if the platoon sergeant and his sidekicks had the brass balls to come into my home and insult my family like that. I was on a mission, and that mission was to fix this asshole today, for the last time. I gathered my belongings and headed for work. Yes, there had been other incidents of his boldness to others, but this is where I draw the line between soldier and family. No one would ever welcome themselves into my home like that and get away with it. That is just wrong, and if I didn't try to resolve it now, it would only mean that this asshole would continue his reign of attitude towards others in the same manner.

I still think, to this day, that Dawn called up to the office, because as I was entering the building from one side, the platoon sergeant was leaving the other side. It was later explained to me that someone had anonymously called and said I was coming up here to discuss the issue from yesterday at my home, and that I was really pissed, and that I was not someone they wanted to piss off at all.

Now for those who do not know me, they had a learning coming and good reason to fear me. Not that I am anyone or anything special, yet those that do know me, and that was a select handful, know that I am well-versed in the art of street fighting. At this point, the mere fact that I wanted "to rip his tiny head off and shit down his neck" meant nothing, and seemed to get the point across. I can tell you that "pissed" was an understatement for me at that particular time and place. It normally took a lot to get me this pissed, but it was an honor thing, and reconciliation at best. The line is crossed when another man enters my home and disrespects my family. I didn't care what happened, or if I were going to jail. I just wanted his ass, and I was going to get it. I was greeted by five military police at the office door and invited into the platoon leader's office to discuss the matter.

"Specialist, please come in and have a seat."

"With all due respect, sir, I will stand."

"That is fine. I was told that you were pretty upset and the reason you see the five MPs is because someone called here saying you were on your way up here in a really bad mood. We also got a tip that you are a martial artist."

"Sir, permission to speak freely."

"Yes, but would you please sit down?"

At this point, I knew from the tone of his voice that I had a legitimate complaint, and that someone was going to be in a great deal of shit over this issue.

"Thank you, but no, I prefer to stand."

Little did they know that my feet were more accurate then my hands, and faster as well. I felt somewhat uncomfortable with the beef patrol behind me, anyway. I needed some advantage if they were to pounce on me; therefore, I was just evening the odds.

"I don't know where you got your information from, but, yes, I do know martial arts, and yes, it was put on the interview worksheet you had me fill out, and, yes, I am very pissed."

"Well I can understand your reason for being upset."

"Oh no, sir. You have no idea how upset I am right now. You, of all people, came to my home and abused my family. They don't work for you, or the military. They are not owned by the military, nor will they ever be. So what gave you the right to come to my home and abuse them as you so willingly did?"

"SPC! I know things were said, and that they were wrong, but..."

"Sir, let me make this really freakin' clear to you people. I don't like the fact that my wife was abused the way she was. I don't like the fact that it happened in my freakin' home. Moreover, I sure do not like the fact that you people had the balls to do it at all. Now, I want an apology to my wife, now, and that is just to start."

"Specialist, let me tell you something right now. You, of all people, are not going to demand anything from me. I will not sit back and be threatened like this, nor will I take you standing there, abusing my authority."

"Authority? Authority? You speak of authority, you punk-assed college graduate. Let me tell you about one thing, about authority that goes well with me: respect is part of what I have given you when I came to this unit. Respect is supposed to be a two-way street. I have given you all respect, but I am yet to see it at all. Yet you sit here and try to lecture me about authority and respect after you and that punk of a platoon sergeant had the audacity to misuse your authority, rank, position, and my family, as a whole. Don't think, for one freakin' minute, that this is going to stop here!"

"Then I guess we have nothing left to say."

"Oh, we have a lot to say, after I talk to a lawyer and file my report."

"Are you threatening me?"

"Sir, if you think that is a threat, then you need to take yourself back to college to be reeducated. Oh, and don't forget to put in your report that you allowed me to speak freely in the presence of these five fine soldiers here, who are taking note."

While leaving the office, I was escorted upstairs to the military police station where I was placed in a guarded room so I could collect my thoughts. My wife came into the room about thirty minutes later. Shortly after Dawn showed up, a lawyer from the JAG office entered the room.

"Hello, I am from the JAG office here on post. Have you talked to anyone besides the unit?"

"No, I talked to my wife, who all this happened to."

"Okay, then, so tell me what happened."

At this point, another officer was not a good sight for me, and I really did not want to talk about anything anymore. What I wanted to do at the time was kick the living shit out of the platoon sergeant for what he had said and done.

I explained my issues to the JAG officer, and to my astonishment, he, too, was truly amazed that it even happened at all. Believing in the fact that he wanted to help us, I continued and ended with the facts that happened in the platoon office. By any rights, the chain of command could have nuked me for sure, and I was definitely way out of line, but they seemed to have different plans for me instead. It was almost as if I were a clairvoyant or something, because the way this JAG officer carried himself, he didn't give off the impression that he was helping me in this matter, but rather, helping the unit cover up a really big mistake.

It is just like the government to cover anything up with a huge silkscreen. I tore that down and went for the jugular. I was not going to talk anymore to anyone here. I learned quickly that no one could be trusted at all. I wanted results, and I wanted them now, just as the commander wanted. When you don't trust in your unit, you later find that you are very alone out there. I was sent to the psychological evaluation board five different times to see if they could get me kicked out, but that act didn't work at all. Hell, the unit even requested a civilian doctor to fly in from the states that specialized in disorders. The outcome astonished even me. The doctor gave me a clean bill of health and sent me on my way. The only one thing that he could gather from picking my brain is the fact that I was abused and was really pissed over the matter. What a complete waste of money and time! Nevertheless, I guess it was not a complete waste. I found out that there was truly nothing wrong with my head. Therefore, I got a free session with a shrink, five different times. I laugh at it today, knowing that I have a level head on my shoulders.

Dear Diary: June, 1994

I am not sure why, but I have had many dreams that seem so real. Strangely enough, they are so real that I can no longer trust anyone or anything. I am so tired, but my body will not let me sleep. I fight the enemy in my sleep as well as when I am awake. I feel as if there is someone watching me all the time; as if to try to find something wrong, to exploit me to the fullest; filleting me open for the world to see my insides, just to shut me up. I feel bare right now; like I have no clothing on at all.

Later in the week, I was called to the CID office, where I would be given an interrogation, and I was asked nicely to put my pen to the paper. Not knowing where this was going, I mentioned the unit gambling through "fantasy football" and all of the other things that were going on. Spilling the beans felt good, but it seemed wrong. I really didn't want to do this, but it needed to be done, for the good of all. This was really not like me at all, and it was a rare thing for me ever to say anything about anyone, but things needed to be made right, and the heat needed to be turned back to those who were corrupt. After going through three years of hate, reprisals, psychological evaluations, interrogations, and attempts to end my career, I ended up pulling thirteen different congressional inquiries on the unit. As I went on with my career, I found that rank does have its privileges. Nothing ever really came from the congressional inquiries as I see it. I was just given the time and space to move onto the next unit and forget it all. However, this would not happen, as I am aware of the processes within the corps, as small as it is. People talk, and I would soon see the true part of this bureaucracy as I entered the next stage in my career.

For the remainder of my time in Germany, I spent a great deal of my time working platoon duty, on the road, or spending time with my new family.

Yes, that is right, my new family.

Dawn was pregnant with our second son, Kyle, at the time all this was happening. I do not know how or what happened to make this tour of duty the most hateful one of my entire career within the military, but it was hateful, and I needed to put it all behind me.

Dear Diary: May, 1997

The family and I will be leaving Germany soon. The unit has since left for Bosnia again, and I was not welcome, despite their desperate attempts to deploy me repeatedly. The determination of the commander to have me killed in the field was not my idea of a good day in the army. However, I cannot prove this, but I did overhear several soldiers talking about it and plotting my final days. It is obvious that I need to get my family and myself out of Germany as soon as possible. Despite all the wants from the family, I demanded that we stay locked up in a small hotel room to avoid any problems that could possible become a reality. The death threats are becoming more and more real, as time grows, near for us to leave. I am becoming more and more afraid that I will not be able to get them out in time; that I will pass before my time on earth is through, and I am not ready to check out of this world just yet.

When the day came for my family and me to leave Germany, we were escorted, by police vehicle, from the hotel to the airport, as if to make up for the mishap and keep me from doing the unthinkable. There were soldiers who believed in what I was doing, and others who saw me in a different light, but as things ended, they would later find that the military is a small place to be when you are a part of the whole problem. Those who knew me cowered away as we boarded the flight to the United States, and I was glad to put this behind us.

Starting on a positive note, I was proud to have served the time I did overseas in Germany. I loved everything about Germany, minus the problems that we had within the unit. Despite the past, I felt like we were going home for sure this time, back home to the land of the free. We boarded the huge airliner that would take us home to the United States, and we could not wait to see the rest of the family. During our stay in Germany, this time, Dawn and I had a surprise for the rest of the family. I thought that being a proud father of one would set me apart from the rest, but I was wrong. I was now a proud father of two. Kyle was born before we left Germany, in the American hospital, and we couldn't be anymore proud as parents. We had made the love of life for the second time, and this would prove to be what we had wanted all this time. I had dreamed of something like this for years; hoping and praying for a family that would break the chain of hurt and bring love back into the chain of life for this family tree. Kyle and Matheuw had the time of their lives on the airplane ride back to the states. Matheuw walked all over the plane, and Kyle;

well that is another story. Like any parent who understands kids and has become numb to the constant crying, let's just say that he cried a lot from the cabin pressure and from being just plain tired. I admit, I shirked my duties as a father. I normally sleep on long flights, and that is what I did most of the time. I feel bad for my wife as she stayed up the entire flight with the boys. She never can really sleep on planes anyway. I did, however, wake up a lot, as the steward would wake me up to get my sons back into their seats, but I fell back to sleep. It is the flight that does that to me, and I couldn't help it. I do wish I could go back and change the fact that I was not there for her much in the past. Things can be blamed on me to the fullest extent, and I have many excuses, but I only wished I would have paid more attention, instead of being selfish and "going balls to the wall" over my career.

During our second stay in Germany, we tried to make the most of our tour by going to the castles and market squares. We would travel for hours to see the small towns throughout the countryside; and the crystal factories, chocolate factories, and bakeries; and the restaurants that were nestled into the wood line that served families, small and large alike. Summers were spent going to Volks Fests and carnivals, or just plain staying home spending time together. This can't be bad to most, but what went wrong? Where did all the pain come from during the hype?

Nevertheless, our trip ended as the plane touched down in the United States. It seemed strange to be home, almost as if we did not belong here. Going through customs was not so bad, and we were actually greeted like human beings for once. Once the customs agent said "Welcome back home," I knew that we were truly home again.

Moving to Texas would prove itself a challenge for the entire family. Dawn did not like the fact that we were going to Fort Hood anymore than the next person, but it was where the next assignment was, and we would have to make the best of what was to come.

CHAPTER 9

Snuffed Out

While reporting to the largest military installation in the free world, I tried to keep an open mind, given the hatefulness that had just been unleashed on my family and me at the last unit. The military police corps is a small enough place, and the world does talk, you know. Nevertheless, this place seemed to feel different. Something about it told me that I would be going places and doing a great deal here. Spit-shined and highly pressed uniforms did what they could as I arrived at the platoon office. The soldiers there seemed very interested in where I just came from and what I had done. I was quickly snatched up by my soon-to-be platoon sergeant and given a ton of papers to fill out. I began to feel at home here in my new military police company, but with some reserve. My eyes quickly scanned the area as I filled out the papers, trying to absorb all that I could. I seemed to gain the feeling of being at home within this unit. I had never done a state-side tour of duty so this was going to be a strange thing for me, and I was not totally accustomed to living in the States, given the fact that I had been overseas for all of my tours of duty. Not sure if I would really fit in, but all the pieces seemed to fit nicely into place. I was quickly taken to the new platoon office, introduced to most of the platoon and given a leadership position. This couldn't be right. I was now in charge of soldiers for the first time in my career. I felt happy being in charge. It felt good to be a part of the top, now. This is where I could show off the stuff that I was made of. Of course, I was nervous, and the soldiers wanted to hear from their new leader, but I just sat back and took in all that I could from everything that was around me. From time to time, I found myself slipping up; however, the military does that to see if you have the potential to excel, and I did not falter in my duties. Finally, given the chance to excel in this career, I didn't want to pass up the opportunity, so I took all the rope they gave me; to hang myself, if the time ever came to that. However, that rope was used for other things, like tying knots in my newfound career path. A good showing of this potential started early in the year 1997 as I was entered into the Fort Hood Nuclear, Biological, and Chemical School. Shortly after that, the unit boarded me for the next step in my career. I promptly graduated the Fort Hood Primary Leadership Development Course in 1998 and 1999 and was whisked off to fight the wars that were to be a part in the destruction of humanity.

Dear Diary: 1998

Sorry I have not written in so long. I have great things to tell you. The family and I finally arrived here at Fort Hood, Texas, and are settled into our new apartment. I have since been to several military schools for education and promptly promoted, along with that. Heck, the military is even sending me to TCLEOSE; that is the Texas Police Academy. This will be a part of the reenlistment agreement that I might be taking. Yes, I have been thinking of staying in, now that my career has moved on, or so it seems. I am still trying to figure out why they are being so nice to me. It is almost as if I were in a fantasy world for the rest to just sit back and watch. The unit is due to deploy soon, and they are trying to rush me into reenlistment, but I am not giving into that at all. I want this to be my special day. Plus, I need to discuss it with Dawn and the kids as well. I want them to be a part of this huge decision. Going to Bosnia doesn't seem all that difficult now, though. For some reason, I seem to be numb inside, and I am not sure why. The past few years have been great. There have only been a few mishaps and close calls, but the rest of the time has been pretty good. Well, I will write again soon. Congratulations to me.

Bosnia-Herzegovina showed me things that I could never have imagined on my own. When we arrived in the war-torn country, the plane combat had landed, and a year-long tour of policing was in store for me. Little did I know that this long year would have more in store for me than just the war. Back home, the wrath of the blood-sucking vultures would try its hand at my wife and family as I fought for this devastated country. Local agencies tormented my wife and took the children from our home after a family member needlessly called CPS on us for something that never happened. It's funny how someone who has never seen your children can just make accusations without checking out the truth first. Remember that third-party hearsay is nothing; but what can you expect from an agency that doesn't have enough brains to show compassion for those who are not even there? I was ridiculed and accused of somehow flying home from a combat zone, hitting my son, and then returning to Bosnia, all within a twenty-four-hour period. In reality, my son injured himself while playing at a local park where he was signed up to play Little League baseball. Assumptions are what they go by, and that would prove to be the last time they would make an accusation against me or my family. Needless to say, I was stuck in this war from both ends; fighting to stay alive, and fighting to get my kids back home while stationed in a combat zone in Bosnia. The courts tend to ignore the other parent, leaving the entire family in torturous turmoil. Things could not get any worse with this going on, or so I thought. While I was chalking up a phone bill of over fifteen hundred dollars in a two-week period to attempt to stabilize the home front, the jet fighters began to fight overhead. The Kosovo campaign kicked off, and we were actively patrolling the borders of Bosnia and Kosovo as the bombs landed only a few hundred meters away. Going into Kosovo was not one of the better ideas, but that was what the commanders wanted.

For those who say you have it hard, try dealing with this, and combat, at the same time. It did not matter where I looked, the devastation was profound. For the towns of Bosnia, every structure was either leveled to the ground, or bullets riddled the brick that held what little foundation was left up, or there was the total incineration of the household that was supporting me as I fought someone else's war. It is amazing how we, as a nation, can police the world, yet we seem to have the very same problems that the rest of the world is having. Kosovo was no different from Bosnia. Everything laid in total waste as we pass for our own inspection, and with that said, it had appeared that our tour of duty ended when the commanders called us from the fields back to the field. Anxiety ramped up inside me as we left this land behind and ventured homeward, not knowing what was in store for each and every one of us. The looks of happiness, worry, concern, and discomfort reached each and every one of us. Not knowing what was in store for each and every one of us was the hardest part as we touched down in the secure airport of Fort Hood, Texas.

The welcome home was short-lived, but fruitful. Spouses and family members came from afar to greet the soldiers once again. It was a private ceremony, and it lasted only a short time as we all stood in our formations, proud, and dead-tired, like zombies. Screams from the crowd pierced the eardrums of everyone that was in the stadium. Once the ceremony was completed, the commanders did not even get the time to dismiss us before children came running up from underneath us to hug our legs. Some children even missed the right parent. They just assumed it was their mother or father, and they wanted them home now. We were like homing devices as the family members swarmed the formation in loving tenderness. Tears fell from all faces in joy, as the crowd slowly dispersed to the doorway and spilled into the parking lot of the night's darkness.

For those who don't understand the homecoming, it is harder than you think. Here you are a soldier, one of the most looked-upon in the world; not knowing what to do in this delicate situation. You have the ability to go off to war and kill, if necessary, and would stop at nothing to free the oppressed from themselves; yet here you stand not knowing. The thoughts tear at you as you ponder what happened while you were gone. What is it going to be like, now that we are back? Will you be accepted or rejected? Will they still love me for me? Is this really my family, because I can't remember much from the past? Will my sex life with the one I love be the same? Millions of questions ran through our minds as we try to make sense of the reality before us. Thoughts of running back over to the war seem inviting as tears ran down the faces of hundreds, starting a trend for you to cry. You feel yourself looking back, unsure if this is the right thing, as you look at the others leaving with their family members, and they also look back to see if it is all real. Will I see them again? Is this truly real? Since you are still on the time zone from the other side of the world, you can't sleep, as those before you slumber quietly. You sneak throughout the house, trying to make sense of all of this; taking in the smells of your home once again; looking at everything that your tired eyes will allow. Is something out of place? Is there something wrong with me? What am I doing wrong? Why am I here? Can this be real? Did I die over there and just come home to this, because it is a comfortable place? No one really knows, but one thing is for sure, reality is a bitch when you are a soldier. Some take it just fine, and then there are those of us that take it to the extreme, because we do not just sit back and let the next person take care of it for us. Maybe that is what my problem is. I had done and seen too much in my time over the years I have been alive. I take things very personally, and I love to get my hands dirty with the rest. Yet, I ask myself. "Who are the rest?" The psychologists say these are all normal feelings, but I like to think different. I am having a hard time with anger management and more. Hell, I cannot even get it up long enough to have real sex. This is not normal. All this takes its toll on me as I make feeble attempts at the impossible and struggle to hold together what little sanity that I have left within my body; to be all I can be.

Dear Diary: 1999

Bosnia and Kosovo was a nightmare. The long, shift hours took its toll on me. I can no longer get to sleep much less switch back to my normal sleep cycle. The things I saw over there were out of this world. Everything has either been shot up or blown up. Every house I saw was riddled with bullet holes or decimated from bombs. From the firefights and the bombs, to the jet-fighter dogfights in the air over the base camps. It all had its own place for fear, yet I did not seem to be frightened over all of this that was happening. I am not sure why, but the numbness inside took hold with deep roots, as the problems back home came to the front of my thoughts. Diary, the feelings I have inside are extreme. I am not sure what to do now. I feel lost and let down. I trusted in the family, the unit, the world, yet the thanks I get from both ends are over the top. I can't say what I want to, so I will close for now. I am too upset and mad to care right now.

The leaders seemed to like me more and more as I took the reins and ran with them for a while. I was later sent to the provost marshal's office to work as the III Corps Army desk sergeant, where I would show off the real talents I have inside. Seeing that things needed to be streamlined within a vast organization, I sat down and designed the "MPOC: Military Police Orientation Course," and then the "DSGT; Desk Sergeant's Course," for the provost marshal's office. This would prove to be just one of the many things that would surpass the many noncommissioned officers before me. The MPOC, after I had designed, instructed, and set into motion, would train thousands of military police, Department of Defense civilian police, security, and foreign soldiers, for years to come. During my stay in the PMO, I quickly moved from desk sergeant to watch commander, and then on to fleet manager. I took the PMO to new heights, along with the rest that had the passion I had. Yet a curse must have been placed on me because someone took a great notice in my talents and I was sent back to the line units. This was a career move for sure, but in the words of so many before me, "Watch your back." I was not sure exactly what they meant by that until much later in my career.

Just to touch back on the PMO fleet manager's job. Since I have left, there has not been another person that could do what I did to the degree that I did. Call it a gift, but I am very good at multi-tasking and seeing the bigger picture when it came to running and tracking the PMO's assets. In this case, the troops had all that they needed, or I found a way to get it. I ran a pretty tight ship as the fleet manager, and you have to be strict when dealing with over 1.2 million dollars in equipment and supplies. With all said and done, I still felt laundered and left lingering with no gratification as I made my way back to the line units. It wouldn't be until later in my travels that I would meet up with the hundreds of soldiers I had trained, or those who had taken my course, saying, "If it wasn't for your advanced course, we would have been lost on the job until we got the hang of the base." The would say that they would not be as comfortable working the base for months until they got used to working the road for a while. Hearing that felt good, and I was glad to help the hundreds of those I did. Here is the turning point in my life as I finish this statement too all of those this concerns.

"You can claim to have done what I did for thousands. You can get credit for what I have done or created. You can take your credits and run along as you did, as I leave with literally nothing to show for it. I say to you, thank you. I did not even get so much as that, but I learned more than I could ever learn in a lifetime. I now know how to avoid people taking advantage of me. I now know how to say no!" There was not so much as a "thank you," given for the hundreds of hours spent away from my family."

As the hundreds propelled themselves to the top of the pecking order at my expense, little did they know my work was just one basis for what was to truly come. Remember the old saying, "What goes around, comes around." Well this is all too true. Those who lied to get to the top are now falling flat on their collective faces. Isn't it a bitch, when you do something good, and most of those you trusted use you and take what is not rightfully theirs? Well, let's just say I believe in the higher powers that work in favor of those who are honest.

Dear Diary: 2001

It has been a while since my last confession to you. I feel empty inside. Dawn has been thinking of leaving me because I am changing my career more than my family life. I cannot blame her, but I do not want to lose her and the career. Please do not make me choose between my career and family. I feel like I am being pimped off to other things in my life, like I have to do it, or else. What should I do? Who can I turn to? How do I let go of one and still have the other? I am not getting the rewards like the others but I am doing a great deal of work. I do not want to complain or be a whiner, but I do not care anymore. All I do is give, give, give, and get nothing in return. What should I do? Somebody please help me.

As my days ended at the PMO and I was shipped off to the basic, noncommissioned officers course in Missouri, this is where the challenges would have their way with me. I did not expect to make it this far in my career, but what the heck. I was here, so I had better make the best of a good thing. It is funny how we are propelled into places that we never really expected to be in the future as life changes itself around us. Making the best of what I had at hand, I pushed onward, learning the finer art of leading soldiers, and in the process, I learned a great deal about myself.

I found juggling a family life and military responsibilities to be a huge challenge, and a fruitful one at the same time. My sons were growing up fast, and I was still playing soldier boy for a job that was taking me places I could have never imagined. My wife was at home alone and in desperate need of passion, tender loving care, and affection from her husband. It was at this point in my life that I saw the reality of the life I had chosen for myself, which was slowly dwindling away as I rode this train of financial burden. You ask how this became a financial burden? Well here it is: I became accustomed to a life of security within the shield of the good life and structure within military arms and security. It is now that I realized that this job was in need of me, and not the reverse. It's funny how the military life makes you see that all you have is a life in the military, and that there is no other way to survive; but I found the escape from the iron grip of the military as a careerist. I had to let go of all that I had seen and done in the eighteen years of service to see the reality before me. By removing the blinders of deception and total mind manipulation, I was now able to see the truth standing before me.

Do not get me wrong; I am not badmouthing the military at all, just the people who are too damned lazy to do their part that they had agreed to. In my case, I was suckered into almost anything for the benefit of others. In the words of the psychologists, there are three types of people. "the wimp, the hard person, and the nice guy." The hard person is the one you can tell nothing to or you will have a hard time dealing with. The wimp is the one who will be nice to you, then stab you in the back. Then there is the nice person; the one you have to protect, because these are the honest, true ones you want close to you all the time. I depict myself as a nice guy, because I live by the rule that I preach: "Be honest to yourself, and it will come back to you tenfold." In my case, I stay honest, because it is the best policy. Once you lie, then you have to keep lying to stay out of trouble. There will always be the simple few who take advantage of the ones who are honest and true to what they stand for. That will never change. "Hey, why work when someone else will? Why break yourself when someone else is stupid enough to break themselves for you?" My legacy goes on.

I have had a great deal of good times in the military, learning a great deal in the eighteen years I gave, and I have enjoyed my time served. I am proud that I was given the opportunity to serve my country, yet, like any other soldier, there is lingering doubt as we soldiers transition back into the cruel world of the civilian populace. This is the part that is very unforgiving, which brings us to this point in time.

I found myself at graduation day, christened by the touch of death that reached from across the world, blistering our lives with self-righteous hate and obviously misconceived religious ways. You ask yourself where you would be if something such as this would happen, and I say I was walking to my graduation. September 11 is the one day that will be remembered forever. The world's tragedy flashes before your eyes. In a moment for once-thriving people, the silence hit and hushed the world forever. It was as if I had no memory of life in me, and the pains of the world where extinguished in a blast of fiery rage.

Have you ever had that feeling when you are driving down the road, and then you wake up, but don't remember how you got were you are now? The reality of that is that you got where you are now, without killing anyone, knowing that you traveled through several streetlights and stop signs. You obeyed all traffic laws, but you seem to wake up and not remember the last few minutes of travel, without killing yourself or someone else? Well that was the feeling that came over me the day two planes crashed into the World Trade Center Towers.

I dropped everything I was doing as I glued myself to the addiction box that brings life to the ones that do not know how to have a life. Oh, no, it could not just happen one time. It had to happen three more times, as if once was not enough. These so-called religious-hijacking, self-annihilating peasants of the underworld have nothing better to do with their lives then to attempt to destroy the lives of others who wish to live in peace and be free. I guess this is something I will never understand; the dumb asses killing themselves and others and for what? Thinking that they will go to the top of the food chain if they kill others? Becoming a murderer or given some form of high-priest status? Well here is a huge clue to those that believe in that shit: you're dead, dumb ass. Plain and simple, you are fucking dead. As I believe it to be, in my own ignorance, killing another is a ticket straight to hell.

From across the world, ignorant, selfish, hate-filled tyrants stirred up the hornets nest a little too much this time. Within minutes, a decision to take the chance that should have been taken years before all this happened. It could have been stopped, yet we, as the most powerful nation in the world sit back and allow things like this to happen to us. I take it for what it is and for its face value. I see the side of one, with a hint of understanding for the other side. As the most powerful nation in the world, we allow our self pity to slap us in the face each time we see the other flinch. Here is a hint to the plutocratic bullshit of the world: "If it seems wrong, if it looks wrong, then it probably is wrong." Our own inhabitants cannot even get it right within department heads, talking amongst each other to get the job done. Instead, they hide among the library of politics and bureaucratic nonsense in an attempt to avoid their true responsibilities. Nevertheless they are still being paid off with your taxes and mine.

Dear Diary: September 11-13, 2001

I cannot hold back the tears. This was supposed to be a happy day for me to remember, as I set up for my graduation from BN-COC at the academy And the drive home would prove to be even more harsh as I return home to my family in Texas and remember death on a massive scale. I cannot believe that all those people are dead; people I never even knew, but shared something in common with. We shared the freedom that those who killed them never wanted. The truth is that I know what this means as a soldier as I stand, glued to the television. This means war for sure. Someone stirred up the wrong hornet's nest this time. Diary, I do not feel scared. That is the strange thing. I feel numb inside, as if I could just kill myself. It seems to be the going thing right now, and there is a saying that goes with what has just happened: "What goes around comes around." "Don't shit on the ones that feed you." And "don't stir up a hornet's nest, unless you can run really fast and not get stung." I know I was wrong for speeding the way I did when I left Missouri, but I wanted to get home now! I knew that time was growing shorter, and that I would not be spending it with my family if I took my time getting home.

Soon, the masses will come and bring the brunt of devastation to a nation of odium and tyranny; or will they? The question still lingers in the minds of many as time passes and deaths of the many fuel the hive; yet it is still futile. Once again, my childhood dreams become a reality, taking me to the lands of loathing and misery.

Dear Diary: August 2002

Well as I said before, my stay at home would be short-lived. I just got orders to go to Korea. I am being hand selected by two command sergeants major, to be stationed in the JSA, right on the DMZ in South Korea. What a place to go for a place of duty! They say that the soldiers there are listed as "Ghosts" because if the North Koreans actually did invade, everyone and everything in the DMZ would cease to exist. I am told that it is a matter of twelve seconds to say your prayers before you would be shot dead by the enemy. This is not comforting to me, but when was the last time North Korea has even shown their face?

Again, I packed my bags and rushed out the door for the airport. I was somewhat excited that I was traveling again around the world, but I wanted to be with my family this time. I was told, however, that I was not allowed to have family members in the DMZ, because of the dangers there. Once again, the loneliness took hold as I boarded the plane for South Korea. It was funny seeing the Korean stewards. I had never really imagined myself in their country, but as I boarded the plane, all they could do was look up at me, smile like they do, mumble something I couldn't understand, and then point in the direction that I needed to get my butt moving in. Polite people, they are. I swore up and down that I would never eat Korean food after the horror stories that were told to me; the fact that, they eat dog and cat. Some Korean food was offered on the flight, but I still took to the American spice that was offered. It seemed to be the safe choice for me at the time. My stomach was doing somersaults as the plane was tossed around in the turbulence.

Hours later, we landed in South Korea, and American soldiers quickly greeted me on the other side. You could immediately pick out the foreigners here. Just about all the Koreans were shorter then your typical American; in average, about one to two feet shorter, not that this is a bad thing. Again, South Koreans were very polite to me. There is just one thing that I cannot seem to get out of my head: the foul stench of something in the air. It did not matter where I went; the odor of defecation and something burning lingered in the air. I am not trying to talk bad about any country or their people, I am just trying to state a fact.

DAMN! It stinks.

Dear Diary: December 2003

Oh, my God, this place gets cold in the winter. Let me tell you, when I say it gets cold, I do not just mean a slight chill; I mean damn cold. The cold goes all the way to the bone. Spending that time in the field was not my idea of a good time. The wooden and plastic chalk blocks froze to the ground, and we had to keep the vehicles running or they would not be able to start again until summer. At night, as we slept in the tents, the wind would blow through the bottom of the tents, setting frost under my bunk. The one gas heater that we did have was just small enough to heat the tent on one side, as the rest of the tent froze in the night. Come morning, the night guards became delinquent in their duties and refused to replace the gas can, allowing the flame to go out, thus allowing all of us to freeze or get a cold-weather injuries in the middle of the night. The next day, I prayed for the sunlight, but only a glimpse came through, warming up the day's air. No one really wanted to work, but it warmed up just enough that I started to move around more, more, and allowed myself to stay busy, taking my mind off the cold.

Dear Diary: December, 2003

It has only been one day in the field, and I am afraid to go to sleep tonight. I seem to be getting used to the cold weather some, but the noises I hear at night are starting to bother me. As close as we are to the DMZ, I fear that the sentry guards will not do their job and will allow the enemy to come into the base camp and get some of us in our sleep. The loudspeaker on the enemy side plays something at night. The Kathusa's, who are Korean Soldier's working for the United States military, tell me that it is the enemy calling the names of the soldiers on our side, telling them to come over to the North Korean side. There is more to it, but I cannot understand it at all. As I go to sleep, the noises they play ring loud in my ears, and putting my arms over my ears does not help.

Dear Diary: December, 2003
Day three in the field, and I already want to kill someone. I am not sleeping well at all. I get maybe an hour's worth of sleep a night now. The food is cold all the time, and it tastes bad, so I prefer to eat MREs (Meals Ready to Eat).

I spent a short time in the DMZ, and then moved to Camp Red Cloud for the remainder of my tour. I was still a part of the DMZ, just on a more important scale. I was given a squad of soldiers, both American and Korean. I took in all that was offered to me, instead of applying the obviously wrong things that were said about Korea and applied my own thinking to it. The Kathusa's Korean soldiers I had took me out on the town and introduced me to their culture. Sitting in a tiny Korean restaurant, I began to learn of the food, the culture, the customs, and the courtesies for myself. A different outlook was given to me, as I learned that not everything is the way it was explained to me by so many in America. It became obvious that the soldiers I had spoken to were constantly in trouble, or had nothing better to do than be hateful of their counterparts. They were guests in this country, and they never took the time to learn anything about it.

Dear Diary: January, 2003

Out in the field again. We have been running missions for over two weeks now. The rain and cold have really started to get to me. I do not think I have a dry stitch of clothing in any of my bags, much less clean ones. Everything is so muddy out here that it is no use to try to stay clean. The noises from the loud speakers play at night all the time now. From time to time, I would wake up and hear someone walking outside the tent, but I did not want to move in the event that it might be the enemy. I was too scared now. I am not sleeping much at all. This is the first time I have laid down in the horizontal position in days. I have not slept in two days now. We had an enemy patrol come within meters of the perimeter in the last few days, and I have been awake ever since. I am afraid to go to sleep tonight.

South Korea became an adventure to me. I explored the small towns and fields as my tour of duty went on, so I could see the entire peninsula with my own eyes and learning as much as I could before my tour of duty was over. The good thing about this tour was that I stayed in constant contact with my family back home through phone calls and the internet. This lessened the stress some, but I still longed for my family's touch. Nothing could replace that.

Dear Diary: March 2003

I have been under a lot of stress from the Kathusa's not doing what I am telling them to do. I am the boss, and they just ignore me. The U.S. soldiers are doing all the work, but the Kathusa's are ignoring me, thinking I can't give punishment to them. I am starting to get hostile towards them and showing more favoritism to my U.S. soldiers. I don't know what to do. I talk to my supervisors, but they just tell me that all I can do is counsel them. This never works. I have counseled them over and over again for multiple things, and they still do nothing to correct the problem. I have my hands tied when working with them. I just give up on them. I don't want to, but I give up.

As time progressed, I saw many hateful and confusing things as the political process came forward with the South Koreans. One day, they would love us being there to protect them, and the next day, they protested for the United States to get out of their country. I cannot count the times I repeatedly said, "Then give me a ticket out of here man." Hell, I did not want to be there in the first place, but I was making the best of it, and I did what I was told to do. The typical, weekly fifty-thousand-person protests in Seoul over Americans being there, the fire bombings began to take their toll on me. There were times that I would be awakened out of a dead sleep to go stand at the front gate and keep protesters from entering the U.S. installation. Many times, I wanted to just run up and open the gates and let them in. Little did they know what waited for them on the other side; until the day a group of them broke through the back gate of the installation, where Korean sentry guards were patrolling. Something just did not seem right about that, but again, we Americans came to the rescue and gathered up their people, all nice and carefully, and escorted them to the front gate to release them. In reality, there should have been quite a few guards fired or brought up on charges for either sleeping on the job or letting them in. Anyway, the point I am trying to make is that protestors got through the fence, because someone let them in, plain and simple. Can we really trust anyone? We, as Americans, try to trust, but the more that our allies play the fake game of being honest, the more we Americans are learning. I know I am not the only one who feels this way, I just seem to be the only one with enough balls to come forward with it and tell the truth.

Dear Diary: April 2003

Again, I have gone to my supervisors for repeated insubordination of the Kathusa's soldiers, and nothing is done about it. I have been told that the Kathusa's do not have to listen to me at all. That they have a direct line to the "Rock Command Sergeant Major," and that they can get me into trouble if they wanted to. I tested that theory as I uncovered a homosexual act and aggravated sexual assault that was going on in the barracks between the old and new Kathusa's. I was told to just let their people handle it, and we, as Americans, are not allowed to know anything about it. Now let me get this straight: these soldiers are put under me, and I am in charge of them, but I am not allowed to tell them anything or counsel them, or even praise them? Well then, these are not my soldiers. Forget them, then!

Forget diplomacy. Forget being nice. We, as Americans, have been nice for too damned long. It is about time that these other countries start doing their own damned work, and picking up some of the bill for the screw-ups that they are also a part of. Not much more was learned out of my tour in Korea other then the different world that it is for the soldier. We are not liked there, and that is that. The food; well, I became accustomed to Korean food, and I started making it and eating it here in the states. It is healthy, and it tastes pretty good, if you know how to fix it; but one thing still stands true: I will not eat dog or cat. The soldiers I had there, well, I'll just say that if they did not want to do anything, then they did not. I had a hard time as a leader there. The Koreans had holidays just about every day, leaving the U.S. soldiers to do all of the work most of the time. In turn, the U.S. soldiers began to resent being there, and in turn, it made for bad relations. There was a lot of adultery going on over there, for sure. In addition, I'd hate to find out just how bad the disease epidemic really is. Drinking, clubbing, or just staying in and watching movies are pretty much all you had to do over there; if you wanted to risk a divorce, criminal charges, or whatever else someone would throw at you. Everybody told on everyone. It was a common thing, and I hated it. I still stayed true to myself, though. Yes, I did open my mouth many times, and believe me, I could have been kicked out for it; but what I said was for the good of the group, and it needed to be said. I guess a taste of true reality was in store for the rest after I left.

My tour of duty ended faster then I had expected, and I already had orders to deploy to Iraq with the next wave. I had not even been home twenty-one days, and I was called off leave to deploy. I guess I was one of the most popular and highly trained soldiers in the army or something, because I was snatched up right out of the twenty-first replacements rolls and brought back to my old unit. This was a plus and a downfall for me. I needed a break, and fast. My family wanted me, but the army wanted more of me, and I needed to be by myself for a few days; but that was not about to happen at all.

Dear Diary: October, 2003

Coming home from Korea was a great relief. In all honesty, I hated that place. I think I am going to have this smell stuck in my nostrils for years to come. The people there are just plan lazy and rude. I hated the fact that there was a curfew on the U.S. soldiers and family members while they were guests there. The Koreans really do not want us there, and I hated the fact that we, the United States, trust someone who loves us one minute and stabs us in the back the next. I am not sure why, but I felt sorry for the place, in a way. Nevertheless, I can honestly say I do not want to go back there, ever. The Kathusa's soldiers that I dealt with were all lairs in one way or another. I caught them in one lie after another, and nothing was done about it. I was hushed up if I went to my superiors. I guess this was for the good of the nation, but I think what was needed was a good, old-fashioned ass kicking. That might get the spoiled, rich-kid syndrome out of them.

Dear Diary: November 2003

I feel empty inside. I am being called back from leave to sign into my new unit. I have been given marching orders for the next month as to what will be happening. So far, I have not spent a great deal of time with the boys or with Dawn, for that matter. Dawn is growing further and further from me, I can tell. She knows what is going to happen soon, and I can do nothing about it. I wish I could just get out now. The pain in my body is hurting enough from the injuries I have sustained over the years that they could put me out on that alone. I have been told that I will be medically boarded if I go through the soldier's readiness program before I deploy, and I am afraid that I will lose my job. I also have a problem with throwing away so many years. There has to be a way to be able to continue my career. So many others are allowed to stay in and continue their careers without deploying and going into retirement. I can see my career slipping away, and there is nothing I can do about it.

Dear Diary: December, 2003

Well, the days are numbered now. I have been told that I should not deploy because of the problems I am having medically. The past few years have shown a great slump in my health. Dawn has become more and more distant, and I think she is going to leave me for sure, this time. My world seems to be falling apart right now as I try to hold onto my career and family. I feel like I am being forced to choose between the two. Why me, Lord? Why me?

Dear Diary: January, 2004

Well, the day has finally come. This is the last night I will be here with my wife and kids. This is the time I need to make up for all the time I have been gone. But this is impossible. Why didn't I spread it out over the time I have been home? Why am I trying to make up for lost time at all? Why is Dawn not telling me something I know she needs to tell me? I can see in her eyes that she does not want me to go, this time. I feel a real emptiness each time I stare into their eyes before we go off to bed.

As I boarded the massive plane that would carry me to the enemy, I thought of the looks on the faces of my sons and my wife as the tears rolled down their cheeks. The hate began to build up inside me with each step I took to the top of the plane. Taking one last look into the cold, dark, night sky before I boarded the plane, I took that potential last breath of United States and Texas air. Nestled into my seat for the long journey, I stared out at the ground as the plane picked up speed and blasted us into the night sky. One minute we were rumbling down the runway, and the next, there was silence. As the plane rose into the night sky and gained its cruising altitude, you could cut the silence with a dull knife. The looks on other soldiers' faces were not that of peace or sarcasm, but anger and the want for payback. I sat awake for most of the flight as the land of the free disappeared from sight. I thought of the looks on my family's face as I was forced to walk away from them, to my potential death. Here, again, I was taken away from the ones that I love for the good of the nation, but we can no longer say that. We, as soldiers of the United States of America, have the right to say that we are the liberators of world; the so-called police of the world. We have the job which no one else wants to do, and they just plain bitch about all the time, yet do nothing to help. If you ask me, I say we have the right to bitch as Americans. We have earned huge bragging rights for all the shit we Americans have put up with over the years of liberating someone else's country. I speak for the millions who care about their freedom: "Put up or shut the hell up!"

I was awakened abruptly as the plane descended rather quickly, and the plane made a fast left bank and then an abrupt right. The chaff shot out of the planes, knowing that someone had locked onto the plane with their radar. Was this to be my deathbed? Was this the way I was supposed to die, going out without a fight? I thought not, as the plane slammed into the runway with incredible force and rolled to the end of the runway. The captain came over the intercom, welcoming us to Kuwait, and gave his sympathy to all of us for having to make a combat landing. I did not know what all the fuss was about; I thought it was rather a fun ride.

It was my third trip here, and still nothing had changed. Glass mirages sparkle through the darkness of the lenses of my Oakley sunglasses, burning holes through my retinas. The stench of the hot desert once again burned its memory into my brain. With a few weeks spent in an outpost in Kuwait, we all fought back the stress and tension of combat and fatigue with what little we had. Letters written would not reach home until months after they were written. The one phone call we did make settled my soul for another day, but it only made me long for home and family that much more. The rains that came during the day covered the tears of anger and stress as I worked my way to the next day, trying to keep my sanity. It did not matter who you were, the stress was there, and no one was immune from it. Three weeks would pass before the convoy would make it to its destination. I was selected for the advance party, but I was bumped for the flight into Baghdad. It was a good thing I was bumped, because the flight was hit by a rocket-propelled grenade as it flew into the Baghdad airport; not to mention that, if I had made the flight, I would have been dead from the mortar round that blasted a hole in the building where my office would have been.

The horror of the unknown ahead crawled across the road in the form of thick fog, as it rolled in with the first part of each morning. As the sunlight began heating up the night sky and the fog burned off, all you could see for miles were sand dunes, which covered this wasteland, leaving to wonder if anything could ever survive within its confines of parched outcast. For hours we would travel, looking upon nothing but remnants of the death of that which once graced the land. Small pieces of burned metal and rubber littered this vast land, as if they were the toppings on an ice cream sundae. As hot as it was, that sundae sounded good right now. Tiny green vegetation lurked in the distance, giving some hope of existence, yet it was merely a representation of death to come if you followed, for it was merely a mirage in the distance. There was no evident live subsistence for miles; it was isolated and stayed at a distance as you moved toward it. Just when you thought life could not possibly exist here in this desolate area of the world, there, in the distance, a child emerged, with another behind that one, then another. These sands breathed life to a terra firma that could not possibly sustain life. Within hours, we closed in on the same mound of sand, that we have been chasing for hours, nearing a distant makeshift camp. This would prove to be the only civilization that would appear out of nowhere, as life is once again respired into the oblivion. I was amazed at the immensity behind such an operation, and how the mass of desert sands swallowed up its intruder.

My stay here this time would be short-lived as I conducted the daily rituals of eating, sleeping, and the grueling work practices of tending to soldiers needs; answering questions for officers and other co-workers; providing security for others I don't even know; and just plain trying to stay alive. The food was good for the palate, but sleep came little, or not at all, as the not-too-distant cracks of gunfire rang out in the night sky, followed shortly by the ever-so-close thunder of artillery. The round landed so close, one would think it was in their back pocket. I do not really think the enemy knew how to aim the artillery pieces. I think they were hoping to get lucky with their hit-and-miss tactics. Some nights I would sit on the dirt mounts, waiting for the rockets to appear. The sky was riddled with death from above as bullets were wasted in haste. As the saying goes, "What goes up must come down." The next morning, we would hear reports of more deaths from falling bullets and artillery attacks.

Explosions around me came closer with every passing night, lighting up the sky like fireflies. Some nights I could hear the occasional 7.62 millimeter round striking the ground ever–so-close by. Then there was not being able to sleep, due to the fear of death and dismemberment by the enemy as I tried to sleep. Mornings found me one day closer to death, sitting in the mess hall, sipping coffee, and eating morning slop. The taste fed my appetite and the lack of desire for my next meal with every passing day of the typical horror and disarray. There were times I wondered if the enemy might be the ones feeding the masses within, as I moved along quickly to my overrated, underappreciated chair. The long walks to the work hall, where I sat in my tiny cubical and performed the tedious tasks of day-to-day, bitch-boy work, for the overly compensated college puppets of the world. They were so damned predictable and too quick to react at the first glimpse of mistake, as if they had never made a mistake in their pathetic lives.

Oh, did I already mention that I never really liked officers to begin with?

It is amazing how the spoken words of the many tend to lash out at you after the fact.

"Do as I say, not as I do."

Ask yourself this one question: how can you have regulations and rules that keep you from having any adverse repercussions come against you for something that cannot be helped? Your friends are there for you when they need help, but when the one in need is you, why is it that your so-called friends are never around for you? So here is a dose of reality: when you need your friends the most, they turn their backs to you, as if to shut you out of the elite group, making you feel as if you had some incurable disease, and now no one wants to talk to you, be with you, or even deal with your issues. It's amazing how much of a true hypocrite we all can be when the need for others is a concern. It brings back the days of elementary school, when you were picked on and left floundering in the devastation of their harsh tongues. It's amusing how it carries over into our adulthood within each one of us. Oh, how true life is, boys and girls; how true life is.

After the first few weeks of the same thing, the long walks back to the hooch did not seem very bad. Oh, who am I kidding? They just plain, outright sucked! The days that it rained, and I would attempt to walk to the shower in my flip-flops and PT uniform were a joke. I would make humor of it as I walked along the pathetic, mud road, sloshing in and out of mud holes, with the hope that I would not get any strange disease from the land that was riddled by death. Just the thought of the freezing cold shower in the dead of winter made the walk back to the hooch seem that much more inviting. Just when you thought you had made it back all clean and ready for bed, you look down and see the mud that splashed up from your flip-flops, onto your already cleaned uniform. Any attempt to get the mud out now only meant you had to go down to the watering hole to clean yourself up again, then walk back to the hooch to find even more mud on you. It was a never-ending cycle and a dismal way of life for the many. The only true time I had to myself, without the fear of death, was when I walked back from work to the hooch in the dark. It was as if there was no one else around. I pretended to block out everything and took myself back home, where I truly belonged. It was at that time that I knew that I needed to get out of there. I began to fantasize that the enemy had breached the wall and were waiting for me in the dark as I walked alone in the dark. I could not feel anything inside anymore. I began to think I was invincible, and I wanted to die. I did not have any fear anymore as rounds impacted around me, followed with gunfire ringing in the air as I just walked on in my own little world. The next morning, I could not remember anything to tell anyone about what had happened. As the nights went by, I would sit on the step of the hooch and listen with my eyes closed, to the sounds of war. Was this my end? Was I slipping into the unknown? It must have been the end, as I began to envision my death; the gore of it all, and how I would be found, alone and lying in pieces from the aftermath. I no longer cared if I would be killed. I just wanted it to be finished with. However, like any reasonable human, I tried not to think about it, as I longed for home more and more. I was missing my son's laughs and the typical fights between brothers; the tender touches of my wife's hand on my face, and the gentle look she gives as she looks into my eyes, peering deep into my torn heart. Yet this would slap me back to a reality that was playing like a movie in real time. The torture was tremendous, as the shells came crashing in, one by one. I sat and waited for the one that would hit me. Bullets whispered names at me as they passed by, but mine was not one of them. Standing up in the face of the enemy, I plotted my own death, but death never knocked on my door. It was not my time, and I teetered back and forth with reality and death. This wound of love and hate was beginning to take hold and spin me out of control.

As day would come and night would fall, repeatedly, I became a victim of combat within myself. I carried myself as if nothing was wrong, but deep inside, I was a total wreck. The pain from the sharpnel that struck my face and hands were left unrevealed to the chain of command.. Many times I thought they would think less of me if I did say anything about the wounds, so I went on without treatment from the so-caled professionals. Daily trips to and from the company have proven to be a chore now. With every trip, your chance of death reached its highest point. The enemy had nothing to live for, so taking you with them to hell was not given a second thought; it was just done. Everywhere you looked, there was destruction, mixed with complete devastation. The likelihood of a normal life for anyone living in this region of the world would take decades of struggling before they could even see the light at the end of any tunnel. This lead me to put the barrel of my own M4 rifle in my mouth so many times and want to pull the trigger so many times; but something inside me kept my finger from flexing and sending that 5.56-caliber round through the back of my head, knowing that it would be days before I would be found, maybe even weeks. The first sergeant would see me sitting on the steps of my trailer each morning and night, but after a while, he stopped saying anything to me at all. I could tell that the war was getting to him, as it did the others. My God, we were all being psychologically tortured, and we did not have a choice.

The rebuilding of so many nations throughout the world is now starting to take the shape of something very unrealistic. True, we are a nation of free people, but when we want to inflict that on the rest of the world, it sometimes backfires in our faces. As the older leaders die off; new, stricter ones take their place, as if to give a role reversal from their society and way of living to ours. More and more, the nations of the world tear at each other, bringing back the days of the cold war and total destruction. Is it true that we will all die from the one blast that will be the end, as we know it? That is a question that we all must answer, and soon.

Dear Diary: 2004

A call from the States came to me tonight with devastating news as I attempted to hold together what little sanity I had left in me at the time.

"Thomas, I was raped."

Diary...I do not know what to say, think or do. I mean, what can you say to someone that you love more then anything in the world after they have just been raped? The only thing I want to do right now is kill the S.O.B. that did it. I tried hard not to grill her daily, but the pain is swelling up deep inside me. God, does it hurt bad. Something was just stolen from me forever; something that no one else has ever known. I want to kill this motherfucker and kill him now. These thoughts are making me crazy inside.

Dear Diary: February, 2004

The chain of command has seen me moping around, and they are getting concerned about me. They seem to know what is going on and have asked if I wanted to go home. The doctors have done an evaluation on me and found out that I was not supposed to be in the combat theater, anyway, for health reasons. I will be processed out of Iraq soon. It might be for the better, but I am now afraid to go home. I feel like I am not allowed to go home now.

Dear Diary: February, 2004

Sitting on a dirt mound here near the back wall of the compound, I can hear the enemy on the other side. I know if I give my position away, I could be shot, so I sit quietly and listen to them setting up their makeshift artillery tube. Just then, a loud thud rings out into the night, and there is a bright flash in the distance. As the next round is launched, I make a break for the trailers, making sure not to be seen by anyone. At this point, I am scared, and not sure what to do. I see a patrol coming up the road, and I run to flag them down. The gunner was itching to pull the trigger on me as I ran up waiving my arms in the air. I told them where the enemy was, and they proceed to the location, popping off a few rounds, then breaking off contact with no one in the dark.

Dear Diary: February, 2004

I had to sleep in the HMMWV, "Highly Mobile Multi-Wheeled Vehicle" tonight. The HMMWV, is a military tactical vehicle that you see on the news a lot. The sounds of the past keep haunting me. My mind is going a thousand miles a minute. The sound of the gas generator sang me to sleep tonight. I cannot get the pain of Dawn being raped out of my head. I do not know if I should be understanding or pissed-off. As the morning comes up I make for the showers before I am seen sleeping in the trucks.

Dear Diary: February, 2004

Rounds came in last night over the palace and the motor pool. It was a very close call, actually. It was only a few meters from the motor pool, in an empty field. My ears are still ringing from the blasts and I wished the dumb asses would learn to aim right, because I just got sharpnel in my face and hands. I just want to die. Last night, I cried myself to sleep again. The pain is bottling up a lot now in my head. I have stopped talking pretty much to everyone. I have been pulled off any work shift, because I will be leaving soon. I am just days out now. Hey, diary...do you think I should go home or do myself here?

When the day finally came for me to leave the region and head on back home to the United States, something deep inside of me wanted to stay, as if I could make a difference now. It's funny how we all tend to relate to something so tragic that, when you have to face it, but when it comes time to be taken out of that situation, you have a guilty feeling that reaches within you, telling you to stay and be a part of it. I don't know why, but I had a hard time leaving Iraq. I had the feeling that I would not be seeing some of my friends ever again. That reality would prove itself to be true, months later, as word came from afar that many were injured and or killed in a rocket attack. Like most soldiers, I thought I would speak out against the enemy that killed my friends, but I didn't. I stood in total silence and amazement. I was asked to speak at the remembrance ceremony, but I could not. I had a hard time even typing the eulogy for the funeral. In remembrance of those who lost their lives for their country, I thank you for your sacrifice and pray for you to rest in peace. You are not forgotten at all.

The long, four-day trip home didn't seem so bad as I started to take in the luxuries that we as a free nation have at our disposal. Just the sight of civilization and modernization seemed to bring me half out of my state of disarray.

My homecoming felt more like a chore for those around me as I picked up five large bags without thinking and walked to the curb where my wife Dawn would be coming to pick me up. From somewhere, anger began to fill my veins as my five-foot-eight frame walked effortlessly to the curb with bags in hand that the baggage handler couldn't even lift without struggling. I am not saying I am a strong man, by any means. And I sure don't work out, so what was fueling the anger inside me? What made me lift the five bags that were later weighed, and came to over five hundred pounds? I still am amazed, to this day, that I even did that effortlessly. The sight of my pickup truck pulling into the airport parking lot didn't seem to faze me. Dawn looked gorgeous, as usual, to me, but there was an underlying hurt within me that stained my heart; a pain within Dawn's eyes would later come to reveal the destruction of this man's love for his soulmate.

CHAPTER 10
Rebuilding

As I nurtured myself back to health through doctor's appointments and with my family, the pain that had still gone unanswered finally came to the surface, as Dawn broke down in tears before me. While deployed to a region of the world away, Jodie came calling for my love, stalking the love of my life, one night, while she was shopping, Dawn was suckered into giving a ride home to a soldier who she thought was an honest person and professional. Much to her surprise, the professional was nothing more then your average, run-of-the-mill, typical male predator. His plan was not to gain a ride home, but rather, a ride of joy with my wife. As I sat listening to her tell me of her ordeal, I began to hate inside. The jealousy and pain swelled up to a degree I have never felt before. It felt as if something had been stripped from me forever; as if I was running naked through the streets for all to see. I sat, motionless, for hours, as the pain filled every vein inside me, plotting the death of this beast. I was a married man at that, who didn't care about the love that was already in place between Dawn and I. He only cared to take away what was not rightfully his.

Knowing this, I began to close in. Shutting out the world for the final blow. I blamed myself for the pain. I blamed myself for leaving the family alone and vulnerable. I scolded myself for the hurt that someone else inflicted on another; as if I were the maker, creator, and protector of the world that revolved around me. Could it be that I was just another average person? Was I truly to blame for the insecurities that had just come true in my world before me? Or was all of this just a test from a dream that I was having, as if I would one day to wake to find the hurt all gone and reminisce how all this was just a cruel joke to torture my mind? But reality tells me different. What is the destiny set for me? Why is it that I have to go through all of this harsh treatment? IS there a higher purpose that I have been chosen to fulfill?

As the torment inside me now reached its peak, I lashed out at those within my grasp. Everyone around me was marked as a untrustworthy soul. I used every technique to investigate the matter before taking it to the authorities, but still, the issue would not rest. I found that the matter would just have to take its course with time. Would our relationship ever be the same again? Why does something like this have to happen to me? Why do I feel guilty after my soulmate was raped? Why do I have to feel like I did this to her? Can it all be fixed? Or will time tear the two of us apart? I sum the past up in a matter of minutes as I reflect back on the past, only to be able to move on.

From my childhood, I felt I was left in the cold. I came from a broken family and constant moving from place to place, seeing my father divorce over and over again, only to feel bad for him and the way his life had turned out. High school was a joke for me. It just seemed like I was picked on more then any other kid in the school, despite the overwhelming popularity for my brother and I. I had a younger brother who graced the popularity field much more than me, I sat alone, having to fend for myself and became a recluse. The military, for me, has shown me many things. It has allowed me to grow and find myself as a man; yet throughout my career, I have found that sacrifice is not what I really needed to do. I gave too much of myself for the sake of others, and I did not get the due recognition that is still due to me. Nevertheless, I have made my choices, and I have to live with them now. Setting aside my family affairs for the career was not a mistake, but a challenge that I needed to take. Could I hold up under the pressure? In my case, I think I have held up pretty good, given the circumstances. I thank all of those who have treated me badly, or didn't believe in me from time to time. I learned a great deal from you all. It was through your mistakes, trials, and tribulations that I am the man who stands before you now; well-rounded and level headed. I can only thank the military for the things I have seen. I have traveled the world, to so many different places, that I can hardly remember some of them. I have graced death's doorstep and learned to respect its wishes. For this, I look at my life and the lives around me in a different manner now.

There are those who thought I was only complaining to them, when I was really showing them their own mistakes within themselves. Am I a god? By no means at all, but I do feed off the very language that is shown in every human being. Body gestures and typical body language are key factors for the way I can read you. There are many more, but I am not a clairvoyant, to say the least.

I am merely human.

I am a man of many talents and teachings, and I give of myself, not to ask in return. Yes, I have given up many times, for good reason; yet I have never quit, because one thing still stands true. I have my sanity and my love for life. Nothing can ever take that away from me. Yet one thing continued to creep up inside me as I slept each night. This storyline that lingered within seemed all too real, as I awoke in cold sweats, screaming out for it all to stop. Was I going crazy, or was this the reality of the times? The dreams that haunt me start like this:

Dear Diary, My dreams are yours tonight,

All life and manmade structures on the face of mother earth seem to cease to exist as we have come to know it. The United States Army and its NATO forces missions have failed the planet for the last time. We cowered down in concrete shelters from the fallout, and were now trying desperately to find what little food and water was left after the holocaust of destruction. This became a challenge in itself. The third world countries having been decimated from the final war to end all wars. During the day, I would sleep, if I could, and travel at night, trying to find what little life there might be, if at all. Images of the dead, friends and enemy, flash before me as I pass by their corpses, lying dormant in peaceful terror.

The graphic nature between pain and pleasure no longer exists. Families are torn from one another in the heat of rage that humanity has created; rage of wanting more, and having to concur with each other, because we all were not satisfied with what we already have. Race, religion, creed, color, and ethnic background no longer exist to this lifestyle. Greed has taken it all away, for a lesser, more undesirable idea of what they might have accepted for their personal becoming.

Determined to uphold the promise that I held inside, I push on in pursuit of world peace. Now humanity has the challenge to rebuild humanity, as we once knew it, but only better than before. Yes, I, too, had a family; a beautiful spouse and two motivated, handsome sons. While sifting through the days and nights during my time away, I would think of them. This would keep me going; keep me sane from the horrors of the army's brainwash. Oh yes, it was brainwash, to the fullest extent that is ever given a name. It is the stuff that the military never tells you, until it is too late; like after you have already entered the military and begun your training, and your life becomes changed forever. You can never be the same person. In some cases, you are better than you were, but in most cases, you are a trained killer. That is your purpose. You kill and move on, not thinking of the good and bad; just get the job done and go home. In this case, it makes you wonder if there is a home to go to now.

For me, though, I have to know. I have to know, for my own self-peace of mind. Not even a week after the blast, I find myself back in the same role of soldiering. I had been training to survive and get home, and I would think of my spouse and kids, and keep the terror of faces that would haunt me throughout the day and night; the horror of not knowing if they are still alive or were spared the mercy of pain and suffering through a quick and painless death. Would they consider the fact that I may have been killed in action and forget me? Did my spouse find another during my absence? Would she even remember me? Would my kids even remember me? Do they still love me? This daily amusement of the ever-changing scene keeps me in the right frame of mind for moving onto the next day. I would ponder all that I see and know and debate the politics of doing myself in with each coming daybreak. Miles and miles of silence pierce my mind. Sometimes it is so loud that I would have to shut my thoughts off to the world. Nothing could even take the place of the pain that I have seen and felt. The undisputed hate and anguish of the enemy lives in me now, and is still alive, helping me to forget the past and start a new life in this new world for myself.

Seemingly ironic that humanity has taught us well; so well, that we forget the fundamentals of life, from the very first day we come into this world; so peaceful, yet still so innocent to the eyes of those who look upon you with experience and knowledge. My mind keeps changing back and forth, bending reality from one day to the next. Rebuilding will be the challenge for those that have survived. Days pass, and I gather the remains of food and water for easy consumption. As if starting once again in the Stone Age, I rebuild from the rubble of the buildings that were still standing.

The most trying of times came when survivors were found in the rubble of some of the buildings. Should I just let them die in peace and spare them the pain and suffering that I am enduring? Yet humanity has taught me different. Some carried the wounds of battle, while others with only minor scrapes and bruises. The rate of found survivors grew, as the radiation depleted itself from the planet surface. Despite all the differences of race, religion, creed, color, and culture, we all found a way to work together, rebuilding the world into the place of peace and better technology that man has struggled to reach for centuries. There was no leader at this point; at least not yet. There were only people working in concert, putting their skills to work for one another. Seemingly, it would be easier just to choose options for the better world of living; a new government to run this new world. But that was not an option at this point. It had become obvious that the world did not need a government to survive, because the government had failed us for the last time.

As time passed, people seemed to take a liking to me, and with the vast knowledge I had, they wanted me to be the person to lead these people into the newest century. Nevertheless, my mind was still set on finding the ones that I love and miss. I still had to know if they were alive or not. Months would pass, as we all restored the standards of living once again. Radio communications soon came back into working order, and we found that the extent of damage is not as bad as the world had expected it to be. Upper-level communication satellites still in working order, as they went into automatic shut down as the war went on, avoiding any damage caused by the war. Medical equipment and computers were easily repaired and placed back in operation, helping those in need of medical attention.

A vehicle factory was seemingly untouched by the blasts. Survivors from the factory begin their work on old plans that were kept hidden for years. Solar vehicles were the vehicles chosen to roam the land now. In the past, human beings had excused this possibility, due to greed for power. The production of solar vehicles made it easy for this new world to move around quickly, in search of more survivors, food, and water. Now, with the ability to reach out to the farthest parts of this land, I traveled to the oceanfront. I found boats of every shape and size awaiting my arrival in the calmest of waters. Not a ripple in the ocean could be seen as far as the eye could see. It was seemingly motionless, as life in the ocean has appeared to be untouched by the devastation. Still, the waters hold the antidote of death of those who drink from it. As time goes by, I seek followers to accompany me to the ends of the world. I planned my route home by way of the waters; a home where sustaining life is still unknown; home, where my family and friends live. Days on the ocean are peaceful, with the present company kept. To pass the time, a meeting of the minds convenes in the hull of this vessel for the making of new governments, factories, medical facilities, and ways of living, as seen in the eyes of all governments combined. A new form of currency is drawn into the plan for the purchase of goods and services. Chores are dealt to each person, each day, to share the expense of living on this vessel.

Days pass, and finally the journey has ended as this vessel reaches the shores of the once-well-known America on the horizon. People can be seen from afar, as the vessel approaches slowly, as if the township was awaiting the arrival of this vessel's cargo that needed to be unloaded. The closer we got, and the more the faces came into focus, the more their faces showed the realism of puzzlement. Who were these strangers, and why were they coming to invade their land? Off shore, the military awaits our arrival with guns and deception, as it has in the past. Had nothing been learned from the total destruction of humanity? Had we not learned from our own greed as Americans? It appeared not, as looting, raping, and pilferage seemed to be inevitable as we passed to once-standing stores and offices.

My followers and I were escorted to a military base for an interview by the now-standing law of the land, but I never knew that it would come to the bare-boned militia. The government that was once known here was replaced with the militia, which is now presiding over the land. Martial law reins in the street as life attempts to rebuild itself here again. The system did not fail me totally, as I am recognized as a former soldier of this land. I am numbered back into the military system and given time to recover. I am assigned to a company and the process of finding my family has begun. I am escorted back to where my family once stayed, in an attempt to find my wife and kids. I did not know what to expect, as the base was hit hard by the terror from the sky. Here I find the answer to my big question as I search for my family: I find Dawn working in a daycare center for children. It is true, they are very much alive. My sons are here, with their mother. Dawn remembered all that I had taught her. The greeting was the most emotional of them all. What do you say after this type of hurt in the world? What do you do now that humanity has begun to rebuild again? A long laugh is held, as I tell her of the king-like status I now hold in the other land. The deafening snores become increasingly louder as my shift grows longer. I wished I were one who was blending in with the harmony of sleep. The stillness around me creeps up from all sides, as if attempting an invasion over my worst fears. The darkness encompasses me, but the most high-tech equipment and some of the strongest men alive today surround me. Within seconds, they can be summoned. Still, I remain stiff with fear, silent to the night at hand. Allowing this much-needed rest to go on unannounced. I continue on with the guard duty alone; just my darkness and me. As dawn breaks over the horizon, man has risen once again from his slumber. Death awakes, and it marches over the land once again, with its stealth-like camouflaged trucks and uniforms, leaving no stone unturned, as we search for the unknown.

The Grim Reaper strikes once again to all those who did not heed the calling. All around was death, destruction, and mayhem. A simple retreat was all that could have saved them from this torment, but they chose to push on, as though in a card game, wagering for the best hand that will never come. This time, the other side won.

"Is this all a sick dream?" I say aloud to the heavens. I try to search for the reason God has chosen me to remain untouched, unblemished, and unscathed. "Why? Why me?" I ask myself this question. I now walk alone back to the only safe refuge that was left behind before this torturous end of human life. For hours, my mind ran a blank. I try to piece together the lasting moments I once had as a child. I try to remember all the good times and the bad. I try to remember all the once-taken girlfriends in my life and how narrow-minded life was to them. I try to seek out lasting evidence of my wife and two sons. I wonder if they made it through to safety, or has humanity caught up with them, too? The pain in my heart engulfs me as thoughts race in my head about them not being okay; that death might have come to them; that I am truly alone again. The once-happy peace of my life has come to an end, as all will, but with such scarce introduction that not even Einstein can even try to imagine the pain they may have gone through. As I raise my head to the horizon, I see the once-untouched refuge I called home for so long engulfed in smoke and fire. An entire section of building is missing, only to bear witness to the naked insides of what was once home to many. As I get closer, the stench of burnt flesh touches my nose, embedding it forever in my mind. Just as one sensation entered my nose, another one would slam into the first one, creating anxiety and despair. The acids from my stomach race up and down, as I once see whole human bodies lying in ruin over the ground. It is as though no one has been spared for the sanctuary of life. All appears to have been devastated. I enter my once-intact barracks and lower my tired restless body onto a semi-clean bunk, close to where I once laid my head and called home. Only for a moment did my mind

wander and I was asleep. My eyes can no longer focus, and my feet blistered from walking. My heart is tormented with death and destruction from an eventful day of man's demise, when in reality, it has been a week without sleep. There is no true rest from the death and destruction. "Can this be real?" I ask myself. "Is there true silence after the storm? Is this what man has worshipped, for so many decades and has yearned to find?" My eyes struggle to open as I hear footsteps about me. My body trembles from the inside out, as I attempt to conceal myself by not moving, but it is too late. Whatever it is has found me, lying dormant and alive. I try, but my eyes will not open. I try to catch a glimpse of my certain death shroud. What is this that I feel touching me? Warm, soft hands check my pulse to see if I am alive.

And without hesitation, a supple voice cries out for help. "I've got one here. He is alive. Someone come help me here."

The tension in my body races as more feet shuffle about me. Then I feel my body become light, as though I was being lifted to the heavens; as if I was going on to the new world that was supposedly planned for all who have prayed for it and lived for it; those with the divine right of passage.

For days, I dreamed of gray and white clouds, with a touch of blue sky in the horizon. Wondering what might have become of me after I fell asleep becomes a grim reminder as I begin to wake from my once-entrapped slumber. My eyes crack open to the faint light of this world, as though I was a newborn child once again. The faint blurs of human images come into focus as I emerge from the slumber I have slept for so long. The same voice I once heard before cries out as I attempt to awaken. "Are you all right?"

Finally, my eyes break open as if they were eggshells. All the bodily sap that has accumulated in my eyes has cocooned my eyes shut. I focus on a figure of what appears to be a woman of great beauty. "Could this be real?" I ask myself. "Am I truly dead?" I stop for a moment and think as feet scurry about around me. Is that all life had to offer me? The total destruction of humanity as we have come to know it. It is as though I have been cheated out of life; the one that I had never planned, and in all essence would never have gotten. I am slapped back to reality, as I remember the voice of my savior. I am unable to forget her touch and her voice as she grasps my hand as I come to. I focus into her hazel eyes as they pierce my innards. Her supple lips, defined with curves and grace, smile at me as I attempt to speak, but I am still unable.

"We are in the basement bomb shelter of the Community Hospital. You appear to be in pretty good shape for what you have been through."

I lie there on a makeshift bed of blankets and cardboard, just staring at her as she examines me, checking me for other problems that I might have. She speaks to me, but I am still unable to talk, because it seems I have forgotten how to. My eyes seemingly to follow the outline of her body as she writes things about me on paper. The tightly fitted brown T-shirt hugs her chest as her small breasts peek out at me, standing at attention; just begging to be caressed. Her camouflaged BDU pants hug every inch of her very curvy body as my eyes followed the lines down as far as I can see.

"Caught you," She says to me as I follow the beauty back up to her eyes.

She has curves that ever girl dreamed of, and then some; feminine, silky, and sexy, just like most men like them. Yet she still has a touch of sluttiness about her that turned you on, without the sex. She had thick thighs and form-fitting pants to go with it. It was as though they were painted on, as they fitted tightly to her, displaying every curve that have teased men for decades. She backed away, turned to leave, and replied, with a warm smile, "I'll be right back." As she left me lying there, I watched her leave, fixing my eyes on her buttocks and legs as she wiggled away.

"WOW," I said to myself, not being able to speak.

I was not sure if I was dead and in heaven, or not. My consciousness came back to me as I became guilty, thinking about her like that.

"He is going to send me to HELL," I thought to myself.

Here I am, in heaven, thinking of something that I had not done in a long time. I haven't been with anyone, let alone my wife, in a long time. For sure, I was going to be going to hell for this one. That was the last straw. She went to tell the man that I was thinking this of her, and then she might file a "sexual harassment complaint" against me.

"Oh, god!" I screamed out load.

She ran back over to me, and others followed as I attempted to sit up.

"What's the matter?" she replied.

"Are you all right?"

I just sat up, with my eyes closed tightly, as the guilt poured into my head, trapping me in the days when my wife and I were alone together; the trips home when we stopped to rest, with the kids were knocked out cold in the back seat, and my wife in her tight German dress that I bought for her at one of the German Volks Fests.

We parked far enough off the road so no one would see us as we were making out like two newlyweds in heat. The kids did not even wake up over the commotion that was going on in the front seat. Afterwards, we slept for a few hours, until Kyle's telling us that he had to go to the bathroom awakened us. Refreshed and pleasantly restored, we pushed on home to Arizona.

It was just as I thought, I was out of the frying pan, and she pops back into my head. Only she was as real as they get. She had a smile on her face as the others left, and she was carrying food and water with her. Sinfully sitting down beside me and helping me sit up, I stared into her eyes as I was taken back to my teenage years, when girls were just objects to me.

"For such a small person, you sure are strong," I said to her. "You know, I don't even know your name."

"My name is Dawn," she replied, with pep in her voice.

"So you're a soldier, I take it, guessing from the BDUs and the well-toned body you have?"

"No, I am not a soldier. Actually, I am a medic here at the hospital; at least it was a hospital, before all this happened. Just my luck, huh?"

I laughing aloud, into the air, and Dawn became somewhat smug.

"I don't see what being a medic has to do with being so funny," she replied.

"I am sorry for that. I was just thinking of my ex-wife's name. It, too, was Dawn."

We both sat there, laughing, as she cracked out jokes, saying that, if were we in bed and I screamed out the name Dawn, I wouldn't get into trouble for it.

"I just pictured you in a white dress and high heels, walking the emergency-room ward. You know, the see-through..."

"Yes! I know what you mean, and yes, I have them, too. And I have the see-through white pants, too. They are issued, as all nurses have them. But with your luck, you might not get to see them at all if you keep this up."

"So... I take it that you have the hots for me, huh?" I thought that I could possibly get into the pants of this one, just like back in school.

"Not a chance, tough guy. Not a chance. So what do you do?" she said and looked down at the wound on my arm.

"I am a military policeman."

"I never would have thought of you as a cop. I guess you wear yourself really well."

"What is that supposed to mean?"

" Oh...nothing, really. I was just thinking that you might be a grunt, or something like that. You seem like the outdoors type. You have a spooky aura about you. Kind of like this one guy I was tending to awhile back. He, too, had the same aura about him."

"What happened to him?"

"He died."

"That's not funny, Dawn."

"I was not making a joke. Just telling you the truth. Well I have to make my rounds. Eat all this and drink as much as you can. You're going to need your strength."

"For what?"

"Don't you worry about that. Just do what you are told, sergeant."

"She wants me," I said to myself. She does, really. I saw the way she looked me up and down as she walked away, and then smiled before she turned to leave me to the darkness.

While I was coming to the largest military installation in the free world, faces haunted me as I was taken back to the bodies lying mangled among the ruins. Body parts scattered about, with the blood-soaked sidewalks and streets begging for an end to their flooding. Their voices cry out for me, for the last time, to help them, as I imagine the faces of those who still had a face to see. I tried to imagine that it could have been me lying there, all mangled and dismembered, for God and country. Give ultimate sacrifice for your country, and nothing is given in return to those who gave their life for the price of freedom, while the pain and suffering of the just one can save the world of so many; and for what I ask? For what reason can't the politicians get it through their heads that we don't need to keep sticking our hands into other countries cookie jars when we have problems that we need to fix right here in America.

The morning breaks over the horizon once again, and there is still no change to this devastation. From behind me creeps Dawn as I await the morning sunrise.

"You seem to be doing much better today," she says in a chipper, but settled voice.

"A new day is upon us." I say, pausing for a brief moment as I smell the air. You know we have to find the others."

"Yes, I know we do, but where are we going to start, and who is going to go?"

"We'll all have to start over again, too."

"I know that, too." Dawn's voice in lost despair. "Where are you going?" Dawn asks. Her words were seemingly spoken with fear in them.

"There is a lake up the road a bit. I have to find my family. I thought I might go there for a while and think then move on from there."

Funny how even the most peaceful of things can calm the heart and soul of the restless. It is nature's beauty in the works. Watching the sun beams glare off the blue-green water sets the tone of serenity. I lie back, stare up to the heavens, and listen to nature changing before me. Life's worries seem to pass me by as I close my eyes and dream of my wife and kids once again.

I ask myself over and over again in my head, "Why can't I find them? Why?"

They can't be that far from me; yet something holds me here. Something unwelcome and haunting to the soul keeps me from the ones I have loved and cherished for so long; the very same ones that I choose to live and die for. They can't be that far from me, yet something keeps me here. It keeps me from running back to their loving arms to hold them and reassure them that everything is going to be okay.

It seems that hours have passed as I am awakened by the sound of footsteps. With a blunt nudge to the chest and I wake to find myself staring down the barrel of an AK-47 rifle. It appears that the enemy was not all wiped out in this case. I sat up quickly, trying not to scare the soldier who holds my life in his hands.

The soldier nudges the weapon into my side to get me to move in the direction he desires. We travel for a few minutes towards the camp, and then we change direction towards the main part of the base.

About a half an hour passes, then we come upon a make-shift shelter that holds some people. I can't make them out really well, due to the day turning into night and the distance from us to them, but they look like women and children. Just as we approach the shelter, my worst fears have become the glory of a lifetime of fears. My wife and two boys, along with the neighbors are sitting under the shelter, tied up. The children seem tired and unfed for days. The adults seemed the same, but not as bad. As the kids see me, they call out, "Daddy," but it is faint and in the voice of pain. The soldier strikes me from behind to get me to kneel as he grabs some twine and ties my hands and feet together. I guess that I did teach Dawn well over the years, as she quickly pulls the boys back and hushes them before the soldier is able to figure out that this is my family he has captured and tortured. I hold back all the pain and anger as the soldier forces me to the ground and holds the rifle to my head. My family and friends, in total shock from this, cover their eyes. He begins yelling some gibberish, reaches in his pocket for some twine, throws it to my wife, then yells some more gibberish, which even the most-educated idiot couldn't figure out. He then points to the twine, and then to me as he yelled something. I guess Dawn figured he wanted her to tie me up. I kind of grinned, because I remember that Dawn and I practiced knot tying before. I whisper to her as she slowly passes to make a tight knot; one that I showed her how to do if we ever got into a bind. It is the knot of most magicians. It just looks really good. She ties my hands and feet, then attempts to return to the shelter. The soldier grabs her around the throat and hugs his face to hers. Scared and angered, she trembles, as she is unsure of what to do. The soldier then kicks me over and licks Dawn's cheek. Dawn cringes with disbelief, and then struggles to get away. The boys become enraged, and they run to help their mother get away.

The soldier, overwhelmed, releases Dawn and backs away, raising the rifle towards us all. He then turns away in disgust and perches on a nearby rock, as if to guard his nest. It will be hours before the dark set in, and it will get cold out. Any attempt to escape at this point would certainly issue a death certificate to anyone who tries. Looking from a short distance, I examine my kids and wife. They appear to be okay, but I can tell they are becoming increasingly weak from not eating, possibly for days, and dehydration from not enough or too little water. The others are in similar or worse shape. I have to do something, I keep saying to myself, but the vulture was lurking too close for me to try an escape. I am pretty well-refreshed from the sleep and the care I had gotten from Dawn. If I can only get them all there. As the next few hours passed, I examined the movements of the soldier. He never came too close to me or the women and children, but it was obvious he is waiting for someone as he climbs a nearby tree to use as a quick lookout perch.

When it is apparent he sees nothing coming to his rescue, he becomes increasingly upset. As comical as it is, I use this to my advantage. Knowing that he is also hungry and thirsty, I begin to laugh aloud. With uncertainty, the soldier runs over to figure out what was going on, waving his weapon at me in anger, and shouting some more unknown gibberish, which only makes me laugh even harder. As he lunges forward to backslap me, I move my head, only to be missed by a very weak swing. In light of this, a blunt distraction comes when the kids began laughing aloud. Now is my chance to take this piece of shit! I have worked my hands free, but I keep them concealed. As the soldier turns, he begins to take aim by lowering the rifle at the women and children. I quietly jumped up from behind the soldier and tightly wrap one arm around his twig of a neck, and with the other hand, I grasp the rifle tightly and raise it away from the women and children. My feet are still bound, so there is not much I can do. Using the quick thinking of a trick I learned in my high school days of wrestling, I bring the rifle across his face and lock his right arm with the left. The weapon smashes up against his face, and I begin to choke him out. For a small-sized person, he put up one hell of a fight, with my family and friends watching. It is not the best thing for them to see, but it is all I could do to get them free.

Finally, the one-hundred-fifty-pound sack of shit drops. I hold on for dear life as the last breath exits his body. As the soldier becomes increasingly limp, I quickly jerk his head from one side to the other, as I saw in so many movies. To my surprise, it works. A very loud crackle come from the neck of the soldier, and his body falls completely limp. My family and friends are in total surprise and astonishment from what I have just done, as I let him fall to the ground. Without hesitation, I untie my feet, only to be greeted by my youngest son, Kyle. I pick him up in my arms and quickly move towards the others. Hugs and kisses are passed out for the short reunion. I quickly examine everyone and gather up the rifle and ammunition. The shelter is a good walk away, and night is coming soon. I pick up Kyle, plop him down on my shoulders, and off we all go, quietly into the night. While staying out of site of possible more enemy personal, we skirt what little concealment there is, and make our way towards the main part of the base that we call home.

Hours pass, and everyone seems to be keeping up with me, given the shape we are all in. The stronger ones help carry the younger ones by putting them on their shoulders, while the older children keep up the pace. The whining seems tame to my sore ears, as I am just in awe of finding them. We reach the house by midnight, and are surprised that only minor bullet holes rivet each house. Some homes are burned, but not a lot. I take a moment to secure the home, and I make my way to the bedroom where I find my Smith & Wesson .45-caliber automatic. Now, I am feeling a little safer as they all sit down to rest. I gather some sodas and food from the cabinet, and then join everyone in the living room. I join in on the devouring of peanut butter and jelly. Tired, but alert, I watch over them as they sleep. As daybreak comes, fear wakes the house, with a rumble from outside. I run to the window to see what it is, and to my surprise, it is armored vehicles, trucks, and soldiers rolling into the base. As I went to open the door, a U.S. soldier who was unaware that we were there greets me.

The soldier yells out, "I need help over here; we have a bunch of them."

It is apparent that the troops were going house to house, clearing each residence and looking for wounded. The medics check us all out and give us our clean bill of health.

It is amazing how it takes tragedy to bring people closer together. For the next few weeks, we all try to rebuild our lives, and our families break bread together. As we are unable to find all the answers for what had happened, we all attempted to piece together what little life we have. The units come around looking for their troops, and to get a count. Sadly, not many made it. Less then a quarter of the unit was intact. The losses were great for such a small amount of enemies. I guess it shows the complacency, on our part as Americans, to allow illegal aliens and unwelcome foreigners to come into our borders and make a home for themselves, without working a day or even paying a single tax; hiding out in this vast world called the United States of America. I guess you can say we allowed it. For decades, the enemy infiltrated our borders, waiting for the right time to awaken and strike out. They legally and sometimes illegally moved drugs, money, weapons, chemicals, and ammunition into strategic place, only to wait for the right time to strike out. How easy we, as a society, have become, by allowing foreigners just to come into our homes and take our freedoms that we soldiers swore to defend, which we did, with our own blood, in our own backyard. I am ashamed that we have laws to protect those who break our laws and are not even from our great land; or are not even legal citizens of the United States. Do we stand for this again? Do we sit back and allow terrorist and diplomatic-immunity assholes from other countries come over here and steal our most private of secrets? We need to be asking ourselves these questions. We have all heard about the downsizing of the U.S. forces, and the closures of bases. Ponder this if you will: have you ever thought that those bases might be used to corral you and me one day? I mean, really think about it; for years, the governments have talked of the new world order. What about all the data collected over the net? Once all the global satellites are in place, haven't you given thought to the next phase in the operation? It has been here the whole time, right in front of our faces, and we have been allowing it. Only we can make this change. Alternatively, do we all desire total domination or annihilation? Sure, there are those who would fight, but those few won't be enough.

A growing cult of Satan worshipers is on the rise.

It is scary to think this is a part of the new world order.

Do you ever wonder why, as an American, you are not told the truth about what is being done in space or why you hear so little about it? Oh sure, you hear about all the malfunctions, the delays, the aborts, then, all of a sudden, the launch. What about the newest edition to space; the new space labs for anyone to use? Is this a part of the new world order? We have the technology. Why are we not using it as we should? What are we afraid of? I say it is not fear; it is the government bureaucrats lining their already-golden pockets with even more cash. How nice for them to take what is not theirs from the people who bled for that hard-earned money to make this world go around. You hear so much about how we need to save the A-Zone. On the other hand, we need to recycle. How about more family time?

I remember back when I was in basic training, and I knew that I was making the transition from civilian to soldier. My time came when I was at my last range. You can call it brainwash-

ing, in the best form known to man, without letting you know. With all the sleep deprivation, mixed in with the issues that the drill sergeants have, each second of the day, I passed through the last obstacle of the night, heading for the rifle range. At first I thought it was the night playing tricks on my mind as I stopped in my tracks not sure of where I was. The faint sounds of close-by blasting gunfire rang out in the night and faded to nothing as the darkness of night became pitch black in my sight. Remember the term, "the-deer-in-headlights" look? Well, it happens to humans, too. Other soldiers passed by me, yet I was frozen in time, staring into nothingness. I wanted to reach out to my buddies as they passed, "to continue on with the mission," as we now say in the real military, but this scared little boy remained motionless. Drill Sergeant Jackson screamed from a far, and I knew he was screaming at me, yet my damned legs just didn't move. I was still frozen in time as my internal clock sped up, changing me into a man. "A soldier is what I shall become." Moreover, a soldier is what I am today. My vision blurs to complete darkness for approximately seven minutes, as my past life flashes before me. Childhood memories become locked in the inevitable past. Memories of my once-past mother come to me as I awoke to the sounds of Drill Sergeant Jackson calling my name. With jelly-filled legs, I began to come to, as he placed his hand on my shoulder, asking me if I was all right; nurturing me like Mom used to do. Then the reality of life set in as I failed to answer him, and he began to tug on my arm, shaking me back to this world. I snapped out of my trance and faced the death and destruction that had been drilled into my head. While I gave a "yes, drill sergeant," answer, I was ushered onto the range. Running as fast as I can to the next firing hole, I plunged into the dark hole that would someday save my life. From behind me, my buddy plunged into the hole with me. We grasped our weapons with intense fear and hate inside, as we stared down the range to see the reality of silhouettes coming towards us. Tracer rounds of gunfire came from above and lit up the darkened, night sky with every blast of the weapon. Streamers from the muzzle flash ripped into the bodies of the already dead.

This mixed with the screams of soldiers, and gunfire echoed in the night with every breath of adrenaline. We had become a team as the hate took out the enemy within the night. Life after the military came to be more difficult than traditionally planned.

I was awakened by the sound of an explosion going off in my head, bringing me back into this realm of reality and time, screaming out in a blood-curdling rage, and scaring the life out of the one who laid beside me in a peaceful slumber. Countless hours are spent trying to find a way to make it all stop, but mercy falls on deaf ears as I continue my life within this shell of a life. Sheltered from the reality of civilian life and realism.

As the days go on, I am soon processed from the military, where I now live out my days at home, playing Mr. Mom, and going to VA appointments for treatment. The pain of the many injuries I have now have taken up a great deal of my time. I can no longer do the things I had wanted to do now that I have the time, like play ball with my sons. Countless hours of counseling and therapy barely seem to scratch at the painful surface with a hint of how to fix it all. Yes, the nightmares still come, and on some days, they are worse then others. No form of therapy can fix eighteen years worth of cold, hard hate and rage that linger inside of me and go untreated. Many tell me to leave my wife and get on with life, yet the sensible thing is to stay together and work it out. The funny thing is that I know it will work out as our love grows even stronger together. As I distance myself from the military as much as possible, I sometimes think back on the good times as they come, and then see myself now. Moreover, I cannot count on the many doctors I go to see now, and the countless amounts of pencil whipping, these same doctors have put in my files.

One thing I can see is that the political bullshit follows you to the civilian life. Doctors will tell you one thing and put something very different in your files. This is so they don't have to pay you what you are worth. It's just another bureaucratic bullshit scheme to keep the higher-ups at the top and the lower enlisted separated from reality. If you think I am bluffing on this one, just ask the thousands who now stand in the long, waiting lines for care that never comes. What is even worse is the fact that there is a growing concern that they cannot pay for the mistakes the military has made to the millions who now suffer for the rest of their lives. One thing was told to me, and then I began to realize the bureaucracy even more: "The VA is looking back into the files of those that are not really that injured, just to cut costs." The worst one has a profound effect on the way I get care in the VA or anywhere now: "You are too young to be here and have this many injuries;" or "This much wrong with you." Like that is my freakin' problem, right? I am looked at as if I am faking it, and the doctors say one thing, then type other shit in the files that gets my case thrown out. After fighting enough, I have finally gotten what I deserve, but I still think the millions deserve their day in court, too.

I will answer the following questions for all of you, though: the hate rages inside and is totally uncontrollable at times. I feel very let down and destroyed inside as a person. The dignity has been ripped from the very soul that this shell supports. The trust of another is rare or nonexistent in my life. Time passes, and I want to be the one in charge, but no one will let me. I know I can fix all of this with the snap of a finger. Most of the world has no damned common sense, but what can I do right? The answers to a lot of questions are still lingering are here, but common sense applies to almost everything you do in your life. From the way you have to act and carry yourself, to the pains you have to deal with when someone else screws you out of your own damned life experiences.

I don't endorse this or any form of violence, but, yes, there are lingering thoughts of wanting to just kick the living shit out of all of those who have done me wrong. Do I regret saying that? NO! The reality of facts and truth are this: if you lie to someone or do them wrong, remember that it will come back to haunt you somewhere down the line. A great deal of us don't even think of that before we speak or act, yet we hurt the very thing that means the most, and that is ourselves.

So you might ask, "What did I do to deserve this?"

Well that is something you have to figure out, kids; something that all you so-called educated buffs who think you know what you are talking about try to figure out every day. Let me let you in on a life-secret, people: "The damn book is not the only answer and it is not the only way."

So get over it and move on. There are some things you just cannot explain and the doctors are the worst ones for that.

I now leave you with my legacy, folks: growing old and grey before my time is up. Is there life after the military? Well, sure there is, but only if you want there to be life. I have struggled much within myself, and I think that goes for a great deal of soldiers with mounds of trauma in their life. I have seen way too much for my short time on Earth, but I have been blessed with the knowledge that I have helped a great deal of people with what I have done, and I am thankful inside for that; yet I still long for the love that I left behind so many times. My days are spent searching for those days, to replace the emptiness inside; to replace the anger and hate that rages before me; trying to find some form of love again that I lost so many times before.

Special thanks go to the ones who believed in me the most: my family. Through the countless days and nights that you worried and went on without me being there for you, I thank you, from the bottom of my heart. To those who believed in me for all that I am and all that I achieved, thank you. And to the nation, thank you for allowing me to serve you in our time of need. It has been a pleasure to serve proudly. To the fans who read my legacy, thank you for buying the book, and I only pray that this will help you along your journey throughout the rest of your life. I leave you with something I used to tell my soldiers all the time: "Remember that it is you that makes the difference for you. Only you can change you. Only you have the key which unlocks the doors. There comes a time in your life when you just have to say it is time to let things go, but don't let them go, just because it is the easy way out. Remember that if you lie to someone else, then you are lying to yourself first, and then you have to try and fix that mistake in your life; so be true to you, first, no matter what that other person does. You'll respect yourself later in life."

Thomas R. Schombert
SSG, USA
Military Police
Retired, Disabled Veteran

BUCKET HEAD

By Thomas R. Schombert

Bucket Head is based on actual occurrences that took place over a seventeen-year period throughout the life of a young man turned soldier turned disabled veteran. Read about the torment that took place that eventually drove this soldier to career suicide, even after his career took off. While he was almost at the top, he tells you how and why he gave up the only things that meant the most in his world of adventure and noble work existence; how he gave it all up for the love of one even stronger passion in his life; one that would betray and haunt him forever. As you read into this gut-wrenching, heart-breaking, and haunting story, see if you would have taken the same road or turned a shy eye to the past. Experience the fears of horror as this man, this soldier tries to deal with his fears from PTSD, then understand the reality of it as this man shows you that not everything is worth turning away from, and that life is really what it says it is.

Chapter I

The townspeople gathered again for the daily ritual of high school sports. Young men mangled each other on a field of lines as young girls danced on the sidelines in short skirts and tight-fitting tops. The parents on both sides battled for whose kid was the best on the field. I was a good kid by any right, and was a somewhat popular person in the town. Just about all the girls in the town knew my father or the family, in one way or another. Kim was the town's run-of-the-mill tramp who was always in everyone else's business, for the most part. She had ambitions to be a high-paid executive, yet her grades left something to be desired to get into her college of choice. Kim used something much more desired at the time, and that was her looks. Karen, Kim's little sister, was the town's toy that every male, including her teachers, must have. Karen had the type of look like a typical, prim-and-proper church schoolgirl. She loved to play soccer, and she played the flute in the marching band, but the truth of the matter was that she was anything but prim and proper. Stories began to mount about how Karen made out with the soccer coach. After hearing the truth, jealousy began to mount in my heart. In addition, let's just say I was very quiet and had my fair share of issues off the field. I never really played the sport, even though I was on the team.

After half a season of football and sitting on the sidelines, the coach put me in for the worst play, that would come to haunt me for the rest of my life. All the townspeople were there for that home game, and my father and stepmother sat in the stands, as well. I thought that I would just warm the bench as usual, but the coach called on the one person who did not appear in the games at Catalina High. My younger brother, the jock, also sat in the stands, watching with intensity, as if coaching from the stands. I turned to see the laughter of my younger brother, who snickered me as I made my way to the field huddle. Chris might have been younger, but he was the all-time jock at Catalina High. He played varsity football in his first year and every year thereafter. He was also in varsity wrestling when I was junior varsity. The humiliation set me apart from everyone in the school, but they also knew that I was the romantic one inside, whereas Chris was the hit-and-run type.

Football was not my passion, and neither was wrestling, but I wanted to make my father proud, so I joined as many sports as I could to gain the regard of my father. First, there was swimming, but I did not have the strength to make the team. Then there was football. My younger brother, Chris, was much bigger then me, but I at least tried to make the cut. When I found out I was on the fourth-string cut, I was happy about that. Then there was wrestling; I was junior varsity when Chris was varsity. I was not sure what I was doing, but I seemed to be good at it. I was skinny and fast, making it hard for the others to get a hold on me. Getting back to the game at hand, as the ball snapped, I totally forgot what the quarterback said, and I took off down the field with lightning speed. While outrunning the others on the field, I forgot the most important thing in football. The football was thrown deep into the end zone, and I was eyed from the position of the quarterback. The people in the stands were on their feet, and I was at the pinnacle of the town's glory. Without thinking, I saw the ball out of the corner of my eye and begin to put out my hands. I was untouchable to all players on the field, and the ball passed me, so I lunged to catch it. I fell flat on my face, and the ball was lost for the rest of time. I was no longer the savior of this town's glory. The town never knew that I did not learn a single play in the team's books; I made it look as good as I could. The winning play for the night would not be the glory of this team. It was the one catch that could have changed the outlook of my family and me for the rest of my life, and I blew it. I blew the one and only thing that meant the world to my family and the townspeople. I did not even know what I had done wrong until years later.

After trying out for wrestling, I found that I was not even good at that, either. My younger brother, Chris, took the top reins for everything when it came to sports. After trying my hardest, I was pinned in the biggest state match of the season, and I could no longer hold this body to the clock. Time seemed to stand still, while the clock ticked slower and slower, as the audience begged me to hang on just a little longer. My eyes filled with sweat and tears, and I wanted so much not to fail at just one thing. Looking at the audience, I screened the stands for my father, who sat behind other parents staring intently, but with patience, as he cheered me on. I could see the concern in his eyes as my, back now bent to the point of nearly breaking, bowed to the extreme. I wanted so much to change positions, and now that I jumped to change, the referee slammed down his hand, signaling the pin for my opposition. In the blink of an eye, the stadium went silent as the referee raised the hand of the winner. I turned and walked to the sidelines in shame, without so much as a pat on the back from the coach or the team. I shuffled to the side of the stands, out of sight of the audience, and there I sat, crying in my own shame. I knew this was the last chance I had at really trying to impress my father, and even more, the townspeople.

Two decades would pass before I was able to reflect again on those moments. This is where Karen and I appeared. I was head over heels in love with Karen, but it was all-too obvious that she only wanted me for my inheritance money. I was young and vulnerable, and I began to rebel from the letdowns and turn to the one and only person who seemed to care the most. I ran away from home at the age of fifteen and decided to move in with Karen and her family after they found out that I was living out of my truck. I went from one broken and dysfunctional home to another; the typical suburban American household held nothing special for anyone in this day and age.

Karen and I quickly became the high-school-sweetheart set that everyone placed bets on to getting married after graduation. There were those who tried to separate Karen and me, but we just played them off. Deep inside, I knew that Karen was playing off my newly found riches. I lavished Karen with gifts and fine dining, but all that would soon turn into the biggest breakup in history, to the grapevine of students from all over the town. We were inseparable from the beginning of the relationship, and we did everything together; breakfast, lunch, and weekends. We even moved in together for a while, until tragedy struck. After the breakup, everyone began to feel sorry for me as the news was ushered in about why Karen broke it off. Years before, when Karen was a child, a man in the neighborhood where she lived had raped Karen. It would be known to the town that Karen had fallen in love with this very same man, who was twice her age. The very spark that took me to Karen soon was extinguished, as she took me for the ride of my life, then dropped me off the planet without so much as an eviction notice. The news of the breakup traveled fast. The other students took to the story with great excitement as they began to choose sides. Other studs began to form their election boards as to who would be the next in line to land this wench. This prize would soon be won, as Karen boasted in the glory of new friends of that sort. The breakup took me to a new level of stress that I thought I would be able to deal with, yet time would take its toll on me with great vengeance. I hated seeing Karen surrounded by all her newfound, so-called friends. It would not take long for the obvious to appear before Karen as I pulled out of the limelight and allowed her the space she needed.

The buildup of rage inside me took a bizarre turn, as I took a nasty spill on the front-room floor of Karen's house. Everyone in the house thought that I was playing, and my cry for help went unanswered. Hours later, I woke up on the floor and managed to get to a phone and call 911. As the ambulance arrived, everyone in the house came out of his or her rooms, as if they were interested in what was happening.

Kim, Karen's sister, kept saying to the paramedics, "Oh, he is only faking it. He pulls this kind of shit all the time."

Little did she know that the paramedics already knew that it was not a hoax. I had actually had a real heart attack, and the paramedics explained this to Karen's parents, who stood in the living room in total disgust, amazed that their baby girl would finally be free from the troubling relationship that Karen and I had. As the ambulance took me to the hospital, this would be the very last time Karen and I would see each other for some time . With my heart completely broken at this point, the pain of the breakup took its toll on me and caused a stress-induced heart attack. I knew what was going on, but I did not see it coming until it was too late. I had been sucked dry of my riches, then dumped off to the side like a piece of stale meat. This melted deep into my heart, and head for years to come. When my father was called to the hospital emergency room to see me, not knowing what to expect, he gave me an ultimatum to get help before coming back home. I agreed to check into the small-town mental institution for treatment, after which time I just stopped talking all together. It was as if I became a deaf mute overnight, angered by the letdown of the one love of my life who would be remembered for a lifetime. The letdown was too immense for me to handle. Once inside the institution, I sat alone all the time while group sessions went on. The staff tried to coax me into eating and talking, but nothing seemed to go right for me. It only made me that much more rebellious as the staff tried talking with me.

It took months before I opened up, and it all seemed to be getting better. The pains from the past seem to fade with time as I learned to lower myself to the level of dirt. There was not much left after that, except to go back up. I began to become stronger, and I found new, innovative ways to release the anger and depression of having been raped as a child and the devastating breakup of the one and only relationship that I had cherished the most in this world. My progress went quickly, as I was now attending group meetings in the day and sitting alone in the recreation room by night. My mind was absorbed by a very pretty girl who always smiled at me as she passed to come into the recreation room. She never really said anything to me, much less to anyone else, but she was always polite. A mystical spirit being must have been working here, because every time I wanted to go up and talk to her, something came up to make me avoid the situation totally.

The day finally came for me to venture back out into the world, and the strangest thing happened. The person least likely to say anything came up to me and hugged me goodbye just before I exited.

Silently she whispered into my ear, "I loved you from the start." Then she kissed me on the cheek and walked back to her room.

As I turn to exit through the door, a shout from down the hall came in loud and clear for all to hear. "My name is Candi," she said as she stood in her assigned room doorway, with her head down and a pouty look on her face. I spent the remainder of my high school years at my Dad's house, thinking about what would be the next step in my life, and three years of nothing led me to be the recluse that I am today.

Nineteen eighty-six rolled around rather quickly, and I graduated high school, but nothing could prepare me for the next step I would take. Thinking irrationally and with great haste, I went to the local army recruitment office and applied. I knew that they would never take me, but to my surprise, they needed someone like me. I was one nut mixing in with the other nuts, in a world of pain and hate, and I suddenly did not seem out of place. There were others just like me. My life began to develop a life on its own rather quickly, and it seemed as if something had been pushing me along. The next eighteen years would prove to be some of the most challenging, but I never thought it would take me to another plan of living.

Chapter 11

I had gone in and out of institutions throughout my career. The military loved to cover up the reality with typical statements and false citations such as, "there are plenty like you," or "everything is normal."

I came to know this as medical cover ups; and yes, it still goes on in today's society. Thanks to internet, people can now make a diagnosis for themselves before they go to the general practitioner. This can save a great deal of time in fixing the misdiagnosis, which plenty of doctors face as they claim faultlessness in their profession. In my case, I was nothing short of a wrecked box of parts in my feeble life. While venturing far and wide throughout this world during my short-lived military career, I quickly became tainted by the hatred of the past and my present career. I found no need for the simple things that seemed to bring me pleasure in this world. Being a so-called, highly decorated soldier of the era, from the end of the cold war to the Iraqi conflicts laced my taste buds with something inside me that continued to haunt me, long after I left the military.

Throughout my career, I never truly received proper care for all that I had been through and had witnessed. I think it all started back in high school when I became one of the most picked-on kids of the nation. After the letdown of Karen, the rape from when I was much younger, and my broken life, mixed with a dysfunctional family, I was led to the brink of worthlessness. I felt I had to do more in this life than just be a part of life itself. I needed to be inside life itself all together. I learned to channel the bad into something good, which in my case, worked to my advantage. Of course, I would be given more than my fair share of the workload. I always stayed on the straight and narrow, working my ass off as I watched others lie and cheat their way through the chronicles of their life. I guess that was the accepted part of being in this life. Most had succumbed to lying and cheating to get to the top, while others, like me, had to work our butts off to get a piece of the action. Oh, come on! You know the ones I am talking about; the ones who never lift a finger, yet receive all the credit after you do all the work.

Even though I was in the right place at the right time, I still missed out on a great deal of recognition that should have been given to me; but that was not the case for me. My gift was the simple love that was given by the heavens above. Someone always seems to be looking out for me when the worst of the pain came, except when Bucket Head was around. Take, for instance the time when I was little and I rode my bicycle like Evel Knievel. I thought I could do anything when I was a child. Stupid me, I thought I could jump this one ditch that was more than fifteen feet across, but I fell short and hit the inner side of the hole. I do not remember much, other than my knees hitting the chopper handlebars, and my face grinding into the mound of dirt at the end of the hole. When I came to, there stood my little brother, laughing his butt off so loudly that I thought an audience was before me. As I sat up, the dirt where I had landed was in the shape of a tombstone, with my face imprinted on the mound. In a way, it was funny, but at the time, I was in so much pain that nothing else really mattered. Just as I came to, a little girl with dark, brown hair appeared in my imagination. Her hair went past her buttocks, and she wore a ruffled, flowered sundress with shiny, black shoes and plastic flower barrettes in her hair. She never spoke a word, she only smiled at me, then disappeared from my memory as the laughter from my younger brother Chris rang out in my ears, and I began to come to. At that age, I did not think much of the incident, but later in life, it would play a vital role.

When I was much older and in a new town after the big breakup between my father and stepmother, I found myself doing things just to feel like I was a part of the "in crowd." Between football, wrestling, swimming, track, and now marching band, I had my fill of events in this life. I think I was at the top of my game when tragedy took me over the edge. Imagine yourself trying to show off for the one girl you would least expect yourself going steady with. In my case, I was a bass drummer and she was a flag girl in the Catalina High marching band. She was gorgeous, by any means, and my goal was to take her over the top tonight. That was until the light went out all over the world. Oh, yes, as my world came crashing down once again. I ran to get into position on the field, and an object in my path, not known to me, ruined the night of my life. The closer I got to the object, the more the ringing in my ears got louder. I do not remember much after the fall, only what was mentioned days later in the halls of the school. It seems that my brother left one of the tubas from the brass section on the field. I had tripped when running into position. I could not see that well, due to the very large bass drum that was strapped to my chest. In the process of running and making an ass of myself, I did a terrible face plant into the drum and bent my back so far that those who actually saw the incident thought I had broken myself in two. As funny as it is now, I had knocked myself out so quickly that I did not feel a thing until two days later. Back then, as a teenager, I was limber, thank God. Nevertheless, at any rate, I was laughed at so much after that, that I went into hiding, just to forget. The girl I once adored was never seen or heard from again.

You ask what is so ironic about all of this: jealousy, I think, played a great role in the outcome of this incident. The beautiful teenage lush who adored me as I adored her was nowhere to be found. It was as if she were never there at all. As my face was so neatly planted into the drum and I was taken to another world of thinking, and so was the girl. The girl who appeared before me in my dreams as I remained locked in the blackout was the same girl from years before, yet grown up. I could not tell a single soul about her. It would only draw attention to me, which would start people thinking bad things about me. Therefore, I remained with my little secret for years to come. I had to start thinking of the future, as well.

I began to weigh the options that were placed before me, as I thought back further and further, to each time something happened to me. It seemed that I was going crazy inside, but I could not let this out at all. I was afraid to tell anyone, for fear that I would be locked away in a padded room. The tension began to build inside of me as the thoughts of this girl became very clear to me now, matching the incidents to each other as I too grew up from childhood to teenager. What was trying to be conveyed here? Was this a real haunting that I needed to tell someone about? This is something that was only seen on television, right? In my case, I was not sure anymore. I needed answers, and I was not sure whom to turn to. If I went to the pastor, I might be thrown out of the church. If I went to my father, he would look at me in a different way and would probably send me away. I could not go to the counselors at school, because I knew they would only contact my father and the hospital, as well. I had to find a way to keep this all inside, even though this entire thing was beginning to freak me out at this point.

As I said before, I needed to get out of here. I was not sure what that meant, as no one really does when they say it. Most only think of the now, and they come to regret it later in life. Hell, there were even times that people thought I was on drugs, but no, not me. I stayed away from them, even though I should have been on them. It would give me a reason for all the strange appearances and unexplained happenings throughout my life.

My life after high school became a twisted cluster of the unknown, mixed with trials and tribulations from afar. Torn between the lives I live now and then, I hastily made the choice to enter the military as a way out of this wretched hole that I called a life. It just did not seem like I would be going anywhere if I stayed, working summers as an electrician with my father. Do not get me wrong, it is a very noble profession, but the lights where taking me elsewhere. My feet became too itchy to stay in one place for too long. I needed to venture out into the world and see it. I needed to become something more then what I was. Later on, you will see just how this played a significant role in my life and how it all came back full circle. It was funny that I should say that as I was off to basic training for the military. While lying in bed before lights out, the other soldiers would tell the stories of where they came from or what drove them to join the military in the first place. For me, it was simple, but I never got the chance to tell my stories; not once, not ever. No, I played on the sidelines of right and wrong as I listened to the ever-so-faint whispers rocking me to sleep. Thousands of phrases pummeled my head as I slept the nights away. I dreamed of home, from time to time, and wondered what everyone back home was doing at this point.

I was never really the type to put much down on paper, until now. Even in the absence of family and friends, I pretty much stayed to myself. It was probably a byproduct of all the bullying and such. I sometimes amazed myself that I had not gone on a killing spree, going after all those who had turned me the way I am now.

From the bullying in elementary school, to the endless torturing in high school, the final stab wound came from my little brother. Even though I was the skinny one and he was the jock who towered over me, I still have the thoughts of when I would be very humiliated by the things he and his friends did. It took me back to a time in Germany when I was in a training environment, and a particular noncommissioned officer, who I had looked up to as a private, belittled and embarrassed me to a point of no recovery. To this day, I still get chills from the point that he questioned me, and then asked me to step outside as the entire squad sat in the club in Baumholder, Germany. I learned all too quickly that alcohol and people do not mix well.

While I was sitting all by myself, I was invited to their table; at which time, some of the Joes began the game of "What we know in our life." Being the well-educated runt that I was, I played along and laughed, until they came to me. The incident went as if it were preplanned. Have you ever had that feeling that you know something is about to happen, and then it does? Not déjà vu; I am talking about when you know something is about to happen, and you are the center of the attention, or you are the one in the crosshairs. That is what I was feeling during the time that Sergeant W – as we will call him for short to protect his identity - questioned me about martial arts stances, and he wanted to know if I really knew martial arts at all. With a drunken look in his eyes, he stared me down and lured me outside, where an entire squad of soldiers surrounded us. He lured me into a fight that I did not want to get into. Nevertheless, as fate had it in for me, I was forced to fight a man, and I did not even know why he wanted to fight. I think he just wanted to show off that he knew martial arts, as well. In any instance, he got in his licks, as did I. With the both of us in the wrong place and time, I never found a way to let the incident go.

For years, the rage of bullied hate began to take its toll on me, more and more. At the time, I wanted so much to crawl under a rock and forget I was ever alive. But life had its lessons for me to deal with, and I was handed a card I just didn't know how to deal with. Years would pass, and the same feelings come over me. I want so badly to return to that day, only to kick the life out of that fucking asshole. I want so much to rip his life's breath from his throat, just as it was taken from me that night. I was forced to cower in a small, dark room by myself, where I cried myself to sleep. To this day, I have never been able to face that demon, but I have learned to live with it, knowing I will never see him again.

From time to time, I learned to open up just enough, but I never really did, which came to hurt me more than anything else in the future. Even to this day, I find it hard to open up, or I find that I have to be within a certain comfort zone to be a part of this life. From time to time throughout my career, the past would come up from behind me and hit me in the back of the head so hard that it would knock me out, as if it were real, but I still go unnoticed or unappreciated for who I am and what I have accomplished in this life so far.

Taking the fast trip forward in this life, I will fast-forward you to the section of letdowns and betrayal in my life. You already know some of them as we have traveled, but the worst is still yet to come.

I begin at the highlight of a career change for me. Things are looking up, or so it seems. Promotions come at an alarmingly slow pace. Years have passed, and I have found myself, countless times, standing in the formations where other soldiers are receiving awards for meaningless things. I know damned well that I have done things much more worthy of an award or some form of recognition, from saving the lives of two children in a burning building, to saving the lives of thirteen soldiers who were nearly run over by a HMMWV; not once but twice in the same hour. I guess that was my job as the squad leader, to save the lives of soldiers and noncommissioned officers alike and let someone else take the recognition for it. The funny thing is that those soldiers all received awards, ranging from the Army Achievement Medal to a certificate of appreciation. What did I get for saving them? Not even a "thank you." The one thing I did learn from that was that next time, I would let them get run over by the vehicle, and turn a blind eye to the incident, forgetting I was even in the same area as them. This is a common thing: the good will be ignored for every good deed done. The bad part about that is that the military is going to lose a lot of really good, honest professionals if they keep turning a blind eye to the honest and faithful.

That is my reward. In any case, I took my life to new heights, as you can see, but the rewards didn't seem to be worth their weight in gold, as my life back home took a turn for the worse. My family back home, missing me more and more each day, weighed very heavily on my soul. It had been years that I was gone; not one or two, but ten long years. I was always deployed out of the country or in schools, so I never really got to see the boys grow as I do now. Spending the holidays in the cold rain or sand filled boots is not my idea of a good life. The pay began to disappear before it even hit the bank. More and more, the expense of making my family happy at home in my absence took on a new meaning as I took nothing for myself in the form of comfort, so that my family would stick around long enough for me to come home to them, so we all could be a family again.

Iraq was another story to be told in itself. Jumping from region to region took me to places only the solemnly interested would travel. I dragged massive amounts of gear along with me that I would never use, only to mix it with tons of gear already sent forward. What in the hell could one-person need this much shit for? We never used it when we were in the rear, but all of a sudden, you needed fifty of the same thing. It was great that our country looked out for us the way they did, but you have to question some things they do. What's even worse was that the airports can check your bags, but they see a shit load of soldiers walking with guns, and they don't get suspicious of that. Sometimes these efforts of the mighty can be wasted on the meaningless. Why do we have to be in everyone else's business, anyway? Why do we, as a nation, have to let all the factories and jobs go to countries that are fighting all the time, and our own people have to leave the damn country to find work? It just doesn't make sense. What I see is that we, as a nation, are going to go down the tubes as all the others have. We will soon have no income to feed our families, unless we are all rich. I am taken away to foreign countries for thousands of days, every year, for what? It is basically so I can fix nothing. I cannot see how I, as a soldier, can make any difference in the life of any country, if all they want to do is blow themselves up all the time. In most cases, they try to take me with them. Now there is something that does not make a damn bit of sense. Don't get me wrong for a second, it would not take but the wrong look for me to put a bullet between the eyes of a person who wanted to kill me in any way, especially those who hijack a religion for their own damned cause, which in every case, don't know what the hell that is. How can we, as a nation, liberate any country that doesn't want to be liberated and has been fighting for thousands of years over the same thing? We, as a free nation, will never change them, at any cost.

Now that I have had time to reflect on that, I see the pains of why I did what I did in Iraq, as well as other places throughout the world. Time has a way of changing a person. In my case, it changed me to the degrees of life itself. Candi seemed to pop up at the times when the worst possible things could be happening to me. The unexplained haunted me for years, and now I had to deal with the enemy trying to kill me at the same time.

Bullets whizzed by and mortar shells landed around us. The explosions seemed to disappear in my ears as I walked the dark, camp road back to my hooch, hand in hand with Candi. But it wasn't Candi that I was seeing. It was my mother, Patricia. Mother died years ago, when I was almost five. The child that appeared before me, in any case, was my mother, who seemed to be watching over me, making sure that everything was all right with me in this world. Fear seemed to go away as we walked the gravel road to the front line of enemy fire. In the background, I could hear the faint voice of soldiers yelling for me to get down.

"Get down!"

"Get down on the ground!"

I stood proudly with mother as I watched the streaks of tracer bullet fly around the camp. The cracking of gunshots rang out as the enemy took aim, and every time, they missed me. Mother assured that I would be fine, but something deep inside me began to come up from the depths of hell, warning me to run. The whistle of a mortar flew by with great speed, tearing a whole in the fabric of earth that lay within the base camp. Shaken by the blasts, one after the other, I stood silent and motionless.

As the assault passed, I could hear the voices of the whimpering souls cry out for one another, checking in with every soul who survived the attack. This would not be the last of them, as more were to follow.

Days were spent sucking down the half-cooked food and coffee made by people who couldn't cook to save their life. Small attacks blasted the soil around us during this time. It seemed to be a softening of the soul during the day, but at night, the heart-thumping rage took me for a ride on the train of death. Knowing the enemy was inside the wire, I eyeballed everyone who looked like they came from this region of the world and judged them as they would pretend to be working. I knew damned well that they were pacing off the very next attack point. Others looked out for them as they collected their pay for the day, and by night, they killed for the thrill of something unknown, biting the hand that is feeding them. It was impossible to trust anyone who stood next to you, but you had to try to get along, as I wandered my footprints on their land.

Some nights were rain filled and cold, and others were so hot and muggy that you just wanted to strip everything off to cool yourself. Trying to remain clean was a joke, of sorts. It was their way of seeing if we, as Americans, had what it took to be American, by knowingly putting outhouses in an area they knew would be a trash dump or hit by mortars.

The day finally came for me as I woke to the sounds of an early morning attack. Mortar shells pounded the land around the camp once again, but for some reason, the shells hit much closer than before. Rushing to dress, I hurried out the hooch door, only to see a mortar shell flying overhead and land not far from my sleeping area. Fear raced through my veins as I tried to make sense of the situation. The screams of soldiers rang out in my ears, as the shells fell around me. They came closer and closer, as if bracketing me. Then, all in an instant, the shelling stopped. I stood, motionless and angry at this point. I had been scared awake and pissed off, to the point of wanting to kill someone now, and I hadn't even had my coffee. Walking to the mess hall, I fumbled with my half-bent Marlboro cigarette and tried to light it, fending off the scared soldiers who were still running around in a panic. All the training I'd had over the years began to come to the very front of my frontal lobe, gearing me up for the next attack that could possibly take my very life. I was willing and able to die for my cause at this point. It was at this point that I knew the enemy was working within the wire that I slept and worked in. My blood began to boil as I passed the checkpoint with my military police brassard flashing proudly. The smiles on their faces told me their story in seconds, as I screwed my eyes at them as they waited to come to work, knowing that they were only coming in to plot the next mortar points.

My eyes began to get very heavy as I stood outside the mess hall with a full belly of food, smoking my cancer stick, and drinking watered-down coffee made from the enemy's very hands. It was all that I had to comfort me for a day's pain that would bestow itself upon us soon. I began to have the feelings of psychic sight, as I envisioned the very attacks that would come that day, looking into the very eyes of the enemy soldiers who worked within the camp wire while I passed them for the final time that day. I just had that gut feeling that today was going to be the day for me.

While contemplating going to work that morning, I slowly paced the half-bombed-out sidewalk and roadway. The very people who built them were now destroying the once-glorious castles of Saddam.

The cold of night and the hot days played a very distinct role in the way soldiers react to an environment. Baghdad had an eerie feeling about it as we drove in from Kuwait. The fog covered the roads like a blanket. The trip took days to reach Baghdad, and along the way, we saw nothing but sand. Then, in the middle of nowhere, a child appeared along the side of the road; then another, and then another, without food and water. No parent could be seen for miles. The feeling of loneliness began to come over me, as the site of blown-up military vehicles littered the desert landscape. Huge craters riddled this scorched earth like Swiss cheese in the sands of time. Emptiness filled my veins as we drove into the uncertainty of a potential death. The stories from the media tell a different side of what was really there.

The pains of being haunted took me to new levels, as I now cowered to the depths of nothingness and tried to make sense of my life among the civilian populous. I was now forced to see doctors who constantly reminded me that nothing was wrong with me, or that everything was normal; yet I knew better. My dreams became more deeply embedded in my brain with every encounter, and relapses became more real to me, but I still went to the group meetings at the local VA hospital. With each visit of the group meeting, Candi would visit me through my thoughts. Each night after the thought, I would not get a good night's sleep. The face of Candi flashed before me thousands of times a second, along with the images of friends, peers, and supervisors alike that I knew during each conflict I entered. It was as if time wanted me to remember the faces I had crossed paths with over the years. Ironically, the faces were those of the dead, killed in their youth while doing something they loved.

Dear Diary, 2004

This will be my last entry. I no longer feel the need to go on. I have witnessed the unbelievable. I have traveled the world some thirty-two times over. I have gone into battle with the bravest. I have seen friends die before me. I have been shot, stabbed, hit with shrapnel, and even beaten down by some of my own, but the worst had not come until today. I bore witness to countless awards being given to soldiers for doing the same thing I do now. The ironic thing is that they can receive a Bronze Star for being in an office and working for some general, yet I receive nothing, over countless years of saving soldiers' and civilians' lives, designing programs that change the way soldiers are trained, being wounded by the enemy, and more; yet where is my Bronze Star for being a hero in the face of the enemy? Where is my Purple Heart for receiving a wound given me by the very hands that fought against me?

Today, I took shrapnel to my right hand. I was somewhere I should not have been, and I was caught off guard. I needed my things out of the vehicle in the motor pool, and I was struck by pieces of the explosion that came all too close to the headquarters of the company. I am afraid to tell anyone. It hurt like hell, but I cannot be the one who is injured. I cannot be a failure; no, not me. The first sergeant has enough to worry about without me being a problem child. I tried like hell to talk to someone, but no one wanted to listen. No one seemed to have the time for me, not even the chaplain.

I cannot even tell my wife, and she is someone I can trust. I must say I did a pretty good job of fixing up the cut. Superglue worked great. I guess talking to my buddies in special ops paid off after all. But in any case, I fixed myself and just went on as if nothing happened. The very thought of those who received their Bronze Stars the other day for working in the JMOC, pushing paper for the generals, seems a little excessive of an award. I feel very left out for the injuries that I will never be awarded for. I will never get my Purple Heart, much less a Silver or Bronze Star for taking one for the team, or even in the face of an attack by the enemy. The command sergeant major didn't even want to talk to me today. She seemed to know something was wrong, but when I tried to confront the sergeant major or even the first sergeant, they just walked the other direction. I guess I will never be recognized for doing something good. I at least fixed myself and drove on without a big problem. The scars will be there forever as the reminder of my bravery that I remember, but I will also remember my hate for the enemy as well, as my hate for my chain of command. Sad as this may seem, I wished they, too, would get theirs, but that is too hateful.

Dear Diary, 2004

I know I said this would be the last entry, but I have something to say that I can't tell anyone else. My family is falling apart. I lost my wife. I think she is having an affair. I can't blame her; after all, I am gone an awful lot. The pain is surging through me like a freight train. I feel like my blood is boiling. The first sergeant and sergeant major just bitched out all the NCOs. I am not sure what that was all about. Hell, they didn't even notice the bandage on my hand at all. I don't think anyone did. I guess I am trying to say that I just want to be noticed for something.

I wouldn't know about being at the top, because a lot of people at the top saw me as a threat to their careers and kept me on the bottom step, conveniently shutting me up for the good of the crowd. I guess my truthful upbringing kept me honest, but too honest for the good of the not-so-truthful crowd. Anyway, I want to kill the bitch. I want to kill the bastard that is doing my wife. Every time I leave to do a noble thing, Jody comes calling and has to prey on my wife. Why is that? Why do I have to be the one? Why can't I find the one for me who will keep her damned legs closed to others? I feel like dying now. I tried really hard to pull the trigger in my room tonight, but I can't. This damn vision of Mom keeps coming into my head. The first time I put the nine-millimeter pistol to my head, I pulled the trigger, but forgot that I had not loaded it. After I loaded it, something didn't let me pull the trigger the second time. Oh my God, diary, I just want to die right now. No one even cares for me at all. No one even noticed me today. Not even the platoon sergeant. I held my hand up so he could see it, and he didn't even acknowledge the blood-stained wound.

I am not sure if it was the click of the hammer falling or not, but the sound seemed to be a comfort for me. Diary. I can tell this is the end. I can tell I will not see these people again; not that I want to. I just feel lost and alone now.

Dear Diary, 2004

I am going home after only twelve weeks of being here, with no award, no thank you, and nothing to show for it. I get to go home to a cheating wife and a broken home. I am not sure what to think. I am not sure how to react. I don't even think that she knows I know. I feel cheated out of life. I don't care if this plane crashes. It would be a noble death. Please, God, just let me die right here and now. Let one of the missiles just shoot us out of the sky, so I can be remembered forever as a man of honor, or be forgotten like the rest. Let me be buried with the honors of the heroes. I know that one day I will have to face my demons, but for now, I cannot even face my family.

Months would pass with each visit to the Veterans Hospital in Texas, and it was not until August of 2005 that the final episode of terror would flash in my head from the night before, granting me the diagnosis of Chronic PTSD, among other underlying issues. Finally I had an answer to the haunting that terrorized me throughout my career and newly established life. Before, while I ran with my career, I never really noticed the horrors of my demise. This is due to the constant work that tired me for hours. The punishing, eighteen-hour days tore at me, throughout every bone in my body. Career suicide was not an option, for the most part. Reaching for the "brass-ring" at the pinnacle of my life looked more alluring at that time in my career, Without seeing the potential setbacks and desolation already in place, I lunged forward into the vast darkness.

My travels took me from the coldest, odium-filled mountains of the Korean DMZ to the darkest secrets of the German forests, stretching my brain cells into wreckage of time as I pounded the insignificant sands of the Iraqi desert. I moved to an unusual plain of existence; one ridiculed by a vast majority of doctors and peers alike. How in the world can one man go from being a grand leader to someone so banged-up and uniformed? The beginnings of a newly adorned man began to emerge from this newly found greatness.

One award could not cover the gaping holes of emptiness that reached into my very soul. Countless others received a plethora of ornaments for their hollow acts, yet I would still go unnoticed for my heroism and bravery in the eyes of the enemy.

Among all the rejections that faced me now, it became more and more difficult that I could not explain the horrifying elements that now haunted me. Back in 1992, I began to have nightmares about a black bull that would come in the middle of the night and literally beat the crap out of me as I slept. It was an unexplained ghost that appeared, from nowhere, with the single intent of bringing on the death of this once-great man of honor and prestige. The church even thought about sending over a priest to see about exorcising the demons, but the church did not think it was real enough to bother.

"There must not be anything wrong if we can't see it."

Years of counseling, rapid career decline, and disappointment could not connect anything of tangible evidence to the issues, which drove me to a German Hospital for the clinically insane. I was admitted to the hospital after being awakened by my own screams, gasping for the very life-sustaining air that filtered throughout my body. I did not notice the blood that now covered me. It appeared that this night terror had now become real, as it slashed into my body from beyond.

Neighboring tenants broke down the door leading to my room, only to see an army pocketknife covered in blood lying next to my bed. Everyone speculated that I tried to kill myself, but it was what he or she did not know that would haunt him or her now and forever. Scholars from far and near tried to convince me of my wrongdoing, and they were sure that I had attempted to end my very own life, but in time, the very same doctors, family, and friends would reap the spoils of knowledge that would have them mesmerized for decades. The very same scares that appeared before them would completely vanish without a trace. This unexplained happening would puzzle even the highest of scholars.

Could it be that I wasn't crazy after all? Could it be that I did, in fact, have a real haunting? Could it be? No! Could it really be true that my mother Patricia was the ghost that stood before me so many times? I guess one will never know. The only person of actual knowledge of these events would find themselves called on by Bucket Head. Bucket Head is the demon that comes to me in my sleep. Its dark figure towers over me as I try to sleep. Waiting for me to open my eyes and injest the fear that it spits at me. I had a friend named Paul that I confided in, who was later killed in the line of duty after being called to a domestic violence case. With his being behind steel and stone, strapped to a gurney, the one true friend I had walked to his very own death; "a present to the knowing," if you will.

After weeks of treatment and no definitive evidence that anything was wrong with me, doctors had no choice but to release me to the outside; the outside world where hell could reach me once again, and where the so-called civilized populous glared at me with disgust, as I walked the streets where I was once known as one of the crowd.

I am not sure why, but my dreams seemed to be taking me back in time, and then I would have flash-forwards into present time. It was as if someone wanted me to remember the past, then redo the past, and maybe make some form of difference in my life this time. I was not sure what this meant right now, because I could only remember falling asleep on the plane. Could it be that the plane really did crash with me in it, and my selfish wish for death came true?

I had to change my life, and fast. Joining the military seemed like a righteous thing at the time, as I strolled the cold, concrete walkways of Tucson storefronts, in search of the right job that might be posted in a willing windowpane. Nothing caught my eye except for the sign that I passed a few hours before. "Uncle Sam Wants You," was plastered on the massive glass frame of the storefront. Inside, the lives of many who traveled the world, sat as if they were manikins, and I as my head turned around to see if the signs were anywhere else.

Still walking with my head turned, I accidentally plowed into a couple walking in the opposite direction.

"Oh... Excuse me. I wasn't looking where I was going," I pleaded to the couple as they shot daggers into me with intense anger.

I walked for hours, pondering the sign and the thoughts of the past that now haunted my memories and me. "No one believes me at all. They all think I did this all to myself, and that all I wanted was attention. Of course, how can I explain anything to anyone when I am a screwup all the time? How can I explain the mystery behind the healing that took place, and how only a small scar remained? It all has to be real. There was a knife found with blood on it, and I, too, was covered in blood. The only one who could tell them the truth is dead."

As a grown man now in his late twenties, I had no idea that most of the town had moved away, along with the memories and friends I once knew. While still filtering through the memories of my past, I only remembered the house that I was taken from twelve years before. The town, now deserted dust and rubble, had picked up and moved twenty miles to the south of the flood plain. Passing by the school I had once attended, I started to have flashbacks of the great football games there and the friends I admired. The town I grew up in dwindled in the distance, as the imitation-leather-seated yellow cab pulled away, leaving that empty feeling in my heart of me wondering where the last twelve years of my life went. Nothing appeared out of place, as I fell into a deep sleep while the cab picked up speed and entered the interstate for Tucson. Slowly nodding off in the faded, brown, leather-covered seat, a bead of sweat began to form on my forehead. I started to twitch from nightmares of the past that I seemed to have mastered, but not in this case. For years, I masked the pain, anger, and fear from the doctors at the asylum before I was released. It only appeared to be triggered by the subtle roars of the tires rolling down the interstate, but I remained in a calm state of peaceful sleep. The dreams began to take me back to my old bedroom, where I slept for years. The comfort of home was no longer a comfort of joy as my eyes began to twitch from side to side, and the rushing of dreams filled my head with terror. Images of horror and death clouded this superficial world of irrelevance. Just then, as I tried to wake before the demon of all evil entities appeared, I shuddered in fear, knowing that the path in this dream was taking me right to the demon's front door.

"Wake up. You got to wake up."

I knew that I could wake up, but my mind had taken me to a different place this time, and would not allow my body to wake from this wretched dream. For some reason, this was a deeper sleep than the ones before. The images flashed before my eyes, embedding themselves in the frontal lobe with a much more vivid picture. Unwelcome thoughts flooded my memories with the deaths of those before me. Unable to stop the images from appearing, I now faced the fear of this nightmare. Appearing before me stood a massive, dark shape of a bull, standing upright and erect, as if it were a human being. I cowered away with my arms covering my head as the figure before me began to slash at my forearms with razor-sharp hooves, slashing the very youth from my body and leaving me there to bleed, heart and soul, for the much smaller beasts to feed from. Its eyes were reddish-yellow, like the sun, setting the retinas of my eyes ablaze as I struggle to keep them open long enough to get a glimpse of its obscured face. Its horns, extending out from the side of its head, came close enough to spear me in the stomach with each lunge of the bull, then all of a sudden, a sharp slice cut deep into my stomach on the right side. The horn slowly pushed in with immense pressure, forcing the fluids from my stomach and out onto my lap as I sat up.

"Hey, wake up."

Shaken awake by the driver of the cab, I awake to find myself in Phoenix, far from my once so-called home. Because the cab driver had awakened me, I was not able to fully go through the dream effect, and I woke up, screaming as I did as a child. This was a good thing, as the driver was unaware of the person he was transporting. I was safe from the nightmare for now. I used my hand and shirt to smudge away the saliva dripping out of my mouth and now ran down the window as I sat in half-wet jeans. The flat indentation of the window was planted on my left cheek as I sat up and gain my bearing.

"Come on, kid, I don't have all night".

"All right... All right".

"How much is the fee?" I asked.

"Don't worry about it. This lady got the tab for you."

Stepping out into the dark, I exited the vehicle and stood, and there was an aged woman, probably in her nineties. The darkness and shadows shielded her face from view as I attempted to get a glimpse of her through the sleep within my eyes, the dark of the night, and a glare from the streetlamp. Still half-asleep, I slowly gathered my things and carted what little I had up the concrete steps, with cast-iron railings, to a wooden door with a large, thick, glass pane. I could hear the tumblers in the lock clicked as her key unlocked the door to the building. We entered, and the door slammed shut behind me, as if it were a one-thousand-pound steel door with a spring hinge attached. The wind from the door used my neck as a racetrack as it dissipated in the cold, mildew-filled passageway. A tall, green-colored staircase with steel railings, leading only up, took me to my new home. This hole in the wall with a small kitchen that spilled into the living room and dining area seemed like the cell I had just left. The bed and bathroom both stood separate, looking back at me. This place was empty, like all the others. As the old woman handed me the key, she exclaimed in a crackling voice, "If you need anything, I am down the hall, on the left, in the manager's office."

She handed me the key to my new apartment, and the door closed with a slow and ghostly creak. The click of the tumblers in the door handle seemed to wake me from my dream as I stood in total emptiness. Nevertheless, to my surprise, I was not dreaming at all. Here I stood, wide awake, in this empty hole, alone, with no one to talk to; no one to ask questions of. I sat for hours on the only remnants of what appeared to be a couch, which graced the living-room area, thinking aloud.

"What will I do now? So what happens next? Am I free to do what I want to?" I asked myself repeatedly in my head.

The upstairs neighbors' toilet was running franticly as the neighbor across from them was having the noisiest sex I had ever heard anyone have. The woman sounded as if she was being tortured, but the truth of the matter was that her mate was good in bed. In the distance, a defiant thumping from a car that had the stereo too loud rumbled in my ear as it passed the apartment complex and kept going down the road. The peaceful sanctuary that I had hoped for seemed to be interrupted with all of this commotion which appeared new to me again.

The tension began to build inside, and I tried to remember that I must hold it together and not get out of hand.

Getting up from my new couch potato heaven, I opened the door to my apartment, and just outside the door was my next-door neighbor, sitting on her doorstep, a young, brown-haired girl with silky, green eyes. This very attractive young girl wore a tight tank-top shirt with blue jeans and flip-flop sandals, with flowered barrettes to hold her hair back. Her red, painted toenails and glossed lips gave the indication that she did not do this just to make others happy. She was out to see if I was what she was hoping I would be. The look in her eyes gave the impression that I was all she had hoped I would be, but who can tell in today's society? I smiled as she voiced her opinions to me.

"So, you are the new tenant next door?"

"Yes, I just moved in today."

The smile plastered across her face gave me the impression that she was interested, but I did not want to seem too desperate.

"Do you know of any good food places around here, close by, where I can get something to eat?"

She pointed to the front of the complex, even though I knew where a good store was. I was hoping for a lead, but that line did not seem to work. As she explained to me, rather quickly, the different places around the complex, I gave her the deer-in- headlights look. It became obvious that she was confusing me, so she got up and offered to show me.

"Here, it will be better if I just show you."

"Well, okay then."

Off we went into the nightlights, walking the streets, in search of food. At this point, my manners began to take shape as slivers jabbed at my tongue.

"By the way, I am Thomas."

"I'm Jenna, hee...hee."

Her girly chuckle stabbed at my emotions as the aroma she wore teased my mind into thinking dirty thoughts. The "Daisy Duke" shorts she wore with her pink, spaghetti-strap top made my mouth water inside. Repeatedly, her aroma lashed out at me, giving me goose bumps all over.

"So, what's good to eat?"

Knowing the things I was thinking about this girl, the last thing I wanted her to think was that I wanted to have sex with her. For Pete's sake, we just met.

"Well. That all depends on what you want."

I thought to myself, "She must know what I am thinking." What I really wanted was to hide under the rock we just passed. I had to think of something, and quickly. "How about burgers?"

"I am not really a burger kind of girl, but there is an ice cream shop around the corner here that we can go to, if that is okay with you."

To set things straight, I quickly replied, "Sure, that is fine with me."

For the rest of the evening, we sat in the ice-cream shop, getting to know each other and getting ice cream all over ourselves. I returned to my apartment, only to find the very same loneliness that I found when I first stepped into it. I had to find some things to fill the void inside. I laid on the couch until the sandman came to take me off to dream world.

The next morning I was awakened to the sound of a thunderous wallop at my door. I opened the door, dressed in my shorts, and nothing else. My hair was entwined up into a crazed look that would shock a thousand hairdressers. My one eye glared at the beauty that stood before me at my doorstep, dressed in blue jeans, a white tank top and girly sandals. I mumbled something I did not know if I would regret in a few minutes. I cleared my throat as Jenna pushed her way into the apartment.

"Well, aren't you going to let me in? Or do I have to stand out here all day? Boy, you have a lot of stuff don't you?"

Jenna's sarcastic tone did not sit well with me, especially because I had just woken up and I had not had coffee yet.

"Had a rough night, I see." Jenna asked with a sneer on her face as she scoped me from head to toe, and back again.

I grumbled something as I went to the restroom to take a piss before my eyeballs exploded, and to have a shower before I petrified her with the stink that loomed over me. A thousand questions came out of her mouth as she snuck peeks at the little I did have in the apartment. I could tell she was moving around by the sound of her voice and its position within the apartment.

"You ever think about getting some furniture? A table, or maybe even a bed to sleep on?"

The sinister tone in her voice as she stood in the door of the bathroom began to get me a little worried. Thinking she would try to sneak a peak at me, I snatched the curtain up and covered myself.

"Eventually I will get furniture. I did only just move in, you know," I replied with a more- welcoming morning voice. I stood in the cold shower, dripping wet, as Jenna stood in the door of the bathroom. We both looked at each other, waiting for a reply to my answer. After a few seconds with no response, I closed the curtain and finished washing my hair.

"Do you know of where I might find some furniture around here really cheap?" I asked with utter haste from the shower, not knowing that she had walked back to the front room and rudely let herself out of the apartment without so much as a goodbye.

It would be days before I would see her again in passing. I am not sure if it was the shower, the comment, or the fact that I did not have anything that might have turned her away so easily, but it did not really matter.

I spent the remainder of the month shopping for things to go into my apartment and being dehumanized by people on the phone at my new job. I started working for a telemarketing company, selling magazines subscriptions to the old and worthless. I am not sure why, but I was now doing the one job I never thought about doing. I remembered the phone calls that came into my parent's home, and they were telemarketers. The things said to them were unforgivable. I guess this was the payback for all the times I was a total asshole to them. Nevertheless, I took the job, because I needed the money. I would spend my time off in the hot tub, soaking up the heat as the pain from my cabbage-ear reminded me that I had a dead-end job, as the hot water splashed up onto my half-raw ears. But the reality of it is that it was paying the bills, and that is what matters. My apartment was decorated with a new hideaway sofa bed and a crystal-like glass dinette set. They both came with a matching glass wall unit for dishes and a wooden coffee table. Now that I was styling in the luxury of the totally poor, I felt a little better if anyone were to come over, that is, if anyone ever did come over, guests would have a place to sit, instead of standing or sitting on the floor.

Chapter III

Time doesn't pass quickly enough when you are all alone. A few years passed, and I took on the responsibility of a relationship with the opposite sex. College sweethearts took the best of me and ran out the door, leaving me empty-handed for the wolves. But I was seduced by one sexy lass with a tiny shell of a body. Painted on miniskirts and tank tops with sandals won my heart. The stress also played a great role in my life as I tried to hide the past. I began fighting with myself to keep it all together, and holding back the fears took all I had in me. Then one day, my significant other. Of course, the better half of me, Dawn #2, decided to stay awake and watch me as I slept, only to put me on the witness stand the next sunrise to answer questions about what I was dreaming; as if I had any clue as to what I dreamt about while I was sleeping. In fact, I knew very well what I was dreaming about.

"So, dear..." Dawn #2, said with a snicker in her voice. "What were you dreaming about last night?"

"How should I know, I was sleeping," I quickly replied, as I got up from the glass dining table to get some orange juice from the refrigerator.

"Well, you sure were dreaming about something, because you were tossing and turning in your sleep, and you even talked in your sleep," she replied with a tone that sounded like she was fishing for an answer.

I always hated it when people fish for answers. Moreover, I hate how most woman are; they keep fishing until they get the answers they want to hear. However, if they don't, then they fish until they get it! "So, if I was talking in my sleep, then tell me what I said," I replied with a scornful, but polite phrase, trying hard not to irritate her at the same time.

"Well...you kept saying no, and then you said something about, 'Get away.' Are you okay? Is there something I should know about?" she replied.

I should have seen this coming, as the onslaught of questions bombarded me with total devastation. I could see that she was not going to let this lie until she had answers. Spilling the beans was something else.

"Well, you want answers that I am just not capable of answering, love. There are things I don't even know about myself, but one thing I can tell you is that I have been getting an increase in nightmares. When we met, remember I told you about the war and things that might come up over it?"

"Yes," she replied, with an assurance that my head would not be bitten off if I tried to answer her question.

"Well, this is part of that. I get nightmares and I don't understand why."

"Well, what do the doctors say about all this and the nightmares?"

"Well that was never explained to me before I left the institution, so it is really hard for me to try and explain something to you that I don't understand myself...understand?" I stood with a half-puzzled look on my face and half smile.

"Well, I guess if you put it that way."

Taking the rest of the day for ourselves, we decided to take in a movie and dinner at the one and only Mexican restaurant down the street. Spending time together was our pastime, as we cuddled in each other's arms all the time, even in public. Remarkably, all of that began to fade away as the nightmares came more often. Fending off questions became increasingly difficult. She often thought that I was having an affair. I never noticed the subtlety of things to come, or what would become known as the years slowly rolled by without her in my life. It was as if I had imagined her in my head, and I longed for her presence beside me.

As if it were a punishment for my transgressions, the vividness of my dreams began to open new doors into the realm of terrifying and horrible thoughts. At night, I would lie awake in the dark, waiting for Bucket Head to come again. The sweat poured from my body as the fear swelled up inside, even on this cold, winter night. The neighbors' radio blasted through the wall as they perform their daily sexual ritual on each other. Sometimes it would sound like they were killing each other. The noises would blend into one loud mass of noise as my eyelids closed like heavy, steel lids.

Slowly the sounds faded into nothingness, as Bucket Head crept alongside my bed. The darkness of the room seemed to become even darker as Bucket Head got closer. The tall, dark mass stood over me, with horns as sharp as spears. Bucket Head's skin crawled with fire from the floor where it stood.

His eyes were staring at me, like radiant suns that blinded me, but I could not look away from this horrifying figure that stood before me. Raising its spear towards me in anger, Bucket Head lunged in total anger, sending the spear into my gut, cutting deep into my intestines of life. Bucket Head pulled back as I gasped for air, and then lunged deep into my chest, this time with even more force. The air in my lungs seemed to escape through the holes in my chest and abdomen. Blood poured from every wound as Bucket Head brought in his thrust for the final kill. I raised my arms to try to stop him, but he seemed to go through my arms, and I screamed aloud, "STOOOOOOOOOP!"

I quickly woke to the sweat-soaked bed and the darkness of my apartment. Sitting up in my bed, I looked over at the red, shimmering numbers of my alarm clock. It appeared that it had only taken a few minutes before this nightmare had awakened me up this time. In the past, I would be sleeping for hours before I was startled awake, but not this time. No … This time was different. I could hear the neighbors shushing each other as they tried to listen into my yelling, which had now stopped. I now was the center of attention for this seemingly quiet community of private living.

I couldn't go back to sleep, so I turned my attention to other things. Having showered and dressed, I primed coffee and readied my lunch for the day. I exited my apartment with my head down in shame, as I left for the daily drudge. I could not face a single soul after hearing all that I did last night, and then my own abrupt conclusion. It was more embarrassing than anything I had ever done before. I guess I was talking and yelling a great deal in my sleep, because the neighbors seemed to leer as they passed me, with their objectionable looks across their faces. I sped up to avoid the remainder of the hate, as I reached the parking lot to board my scooter. My day was as typical as the rest, yet I still had a lingering feeling of loneliness about me. It was not that I needed a woman beside me, it was something else. I felt lost without it, but could not put my finger on the subject yet.

Typing notes into the computer all day seemed like a chore for the mundane, as I sat, strapped into my headset and my computer-based cubical. The walls seemed to be getting smaller as the day went on. I prayed for my lunch break to come quicker each day, as the rotating timer on the wall counted down the minutes. The only relief I did get from the day's tediousness was the data plunger, who stood at her station, feeding calls to us as we ended each one. From time to time, she wore a pink miniskirt that would tell what religion she was. I think she did that on the days of her evaluation, or when the big bosses were in town, thinking they would pay her any mind so that she might keep her job just one more day. The funny thing is that they never came to our section of the building. She tried so hard to squat down with her legs closed, like a good little girl, but she never noticed that I was always paying attention. She had the most incredible legs I had ever seen, and she tried so hard to impress everyone but herself each day. I felt rather sorry for her, as she would have to crawl under the tables to adjust the paper feed to the printer machines. One time, her miniskirt even snapped up over her bottom, revealing all underneath. Let me tell you, I knew from then on out that she never wore any panties, just stockings with a hole in the right, lower buttocks cheek. After that fateful day, I never looked at her the same. I felt guilty about looking at her the way I did, as if undressing her from top to bottom. Now I felt ashamed I did that. I am not sure why, but weeks later, she disappeared from the roll books within the big business sector, never to return.

The day ended all too quickly, and I was on my way back to the dungeon. My sinister pungent, squalor of a life that I called home seemed to consume all of me every time I walked through its doors. I knew that the time would come for me to fall asleep and face the demon in the darkness again.

Cannibal Boy

By Thomas R. Schombert

Loneliness only comes when you are not feeling at the top of your game. Have you ever caught yourself trying to figure out the answers for yourself, only to find that you tend to screw it all up? This does not mean that you are insane, or that you need any immediate help; it is only a suggestion in your mind that is saying you need to solicit the help of those around you. No one can do everything on their own. It takes a great deal of society, intermingling, to create the world that revolves around each and every one of us. Remember this, "Loneliness does come with a price." I know this, firsthand, from experience.

Remember that girl I had talked about in the beginning of *Diaries of a Soldier*, and then in *Bucket Head*? Here is where you become enlightened to the other side. That "ghost" was actually my mother, who died when I was about five. She appeared to me, as a protector, if you will. Now, there are some of you out there that do not believe in ghosts, spirits, or the other side. That is okay. I will not suggest that this is the only explanation, either, but to me, I saw it as my mother, calling to me from the other side and helping me along the way during tough times. At first, it seemed strange, but as time went on and I became older, I began to understand the real reason behind this ghost who followed me throughout life. There were so many times that I missed the warning signs, but my guardian angel did not leave me.

Throughout my lifetime, I have had both good and bad things. Of course, this is part of life itself, but I feel that, in my case, I have been dealt a raw deal, throughout the countless years of abuse from childhood from neighborhood kids and a cynical step-mother, to broken relationships and rejection, and on to military life. I guess you can say that I was a typical candidate for all that had happened to me, and why I committed career suicide. I nearly took my life for real over a course of twenty-five years. Now that I am thirty-nine years old, I deliberate the remainder of my life with one goal in mind: to regain what is rightfully mine. Whether or not this will happen in this lifetime remains to be seen, but I will give it one hell of a shot.

Going back in time, I remember the rape as the base foundation for the problems that came later in life. I held back my fears and kept them locked away for years, with the anger for such a violent crime. I do not know the fate of the hateful ones, but I now show pity on their souls from the wisdom of my sorrows within the past.

With the death of my mother as a child, I felt left behind in a sea of hopelessness, as life continued on. I remember so much from back then, even though I was so very young. I am not sure why, but it seems okay, now that I visit my mothers grave each time I return to Arizona. I make it a major point, before anything else in my life. There, beside my mother, lies my grandmother and father, as if they are protectors of her shell. With their beauty in stasis, I wander away from the gravesite to visit the still-tormented family members for the week that I have each time I return to Arizona.

I guess living in Texas is the only way I can get away from the pain and memories of the past. I will only return when I am ready to return and face the demons of my past. With time, I feel more and more comfortable returning, but I have no need to move back there for the long stay. It is as if that chapter of my life has closed, and I have been able to move on and start out fresh. But as fate would have it, I still have lingering issues to contend with, as I quibble over the obvious wrongdoings of those I used to work for; the quibbling girlfriends and constant family bickering that takes place every time I return for a visit. I am amazed at how difficult the world can really be, and I use family issues and past relationships as results of the pains of my life. I have learned from others' mistakes and have taken them to heart.

Haven't you ever wondered why you can seem to be at the top of your game, but others are still living in the Stone Age? A good example of this is when my family and friends call on me for their computer issues. I try to explain how to fix it over the phone. At times, I have tried to fix it when I have visited, but they never want me to look at their computer, even though they know I have the gifted skills and knowledge of computer geeks. Instead, they always confide in someone else, who is going to charge them an arm and a leg for doing the same thing I would do for nothing. Well, I say, pay for it, then. I am tired of playing the same old games. It is almost as if they are questioning my ability to know what I know. Therefore, in return, I have stopped giving advice and have started living my life.

I never was much of a "go along" person. I always stayed on the path of "doing the right thing over the wrong." This was something that was obviously taught to me by my childhood and my strict, Roman Catholic upbringing.

My days off were spent in solitude, quibbling over what had been done wrong to me each day of my life. Why did all this have to happen to me? Why was I the target of someone else's humor? Why did God choose me to go through all this pain and torment throughout my life? The man himself would only answer these questions and more when it was time. For now, this is not the time to have those answers; however, I almost got those answers when I attempted suicide so many times throughout my life. And with each attempt, I gained that much more respect for the unknown, and I allowed myself the time to heal from the pain of death and anger throughout my lifetime, so far.

We traveling from one broken home to another, as my father remarried, and then remarried again, moving us from one house to another; from one town to another. Father was not there much, as he had to work, just to keep food on the table and give the spoils of life to his beloved children. I now gained great respect for my father, as I see myself struggling to feed my very own family in this society of materialistic items and gadgetry. However, though I am spoiled by the hatred of the materialistic items, I now spoil my children with the very same hatred. Society has a way of doing that. The pain of seeing my father as an alcoholic who destroyed the very foundation he stood on led me to an understanding of self-hatred. Father never had the chances I have been afforded and the levels of help that I have received. In a way, I feel responsible for his pain.

After the house fire, then moving, and changing schools so many times over, I was never really known as a normal child anymore; but looking back now, I see the long-term effects of this. I took it in a way that allowed me to better understand it when I grew up. Later in life, I am not sure if that was the purpose, but life itself has a way of passing on some pretty subtle signs as we grow older and we gain the wisdom of the elders. Of course, not all of our elders are of the upstanding type, but we have to make do with what we are given.

As I grew older and gained some wisdom, I found that problems along the way tended to just knock your "pee-pee" into the dirt. As the old drill sergeant used to sing to us: "Don't let your dingle dangle, dangle in the dirt."

The rejections of the many came in my younger years, as I grew through the ranks of the military. What happened in my adolescent years paled in comparison to what happened in military life. Drill sergeants have to train you to be something you would never think of being. The only downfall to that, is that the military doesn't effectively train a soldier to become a civilian again, as if to let the killer out of its cage to fend for itself now that it has been paroled.

If this is starting to sound familiar, let me know. Constantly, I would be picked on, only because I seemed vulnerable because of my size and how smart I really was. I was, what they call in today's society, "a geek." Name-calling is only the beginning, folks. Bullying in the home has life consequences, as does school bullying, to which I fell victim a great deal. The humiliation set in even more, as my pride was taken from me. Using my younger brother, who was much bigger then me, to fend off the fights that would have taken place over the course of my adolescent years, was embarrassing. I fell prey to the abuse of children who wanted to be part of the "in crowd," by trying to drag down. I rebelled in the most profound ways, and I thank myself for that everyday now. The so-called popular ones are now falling pray to life's little secrets. I guess they should not have done all those drugs, along with the drinking at such a young age. It is now catching up with them. I feel glad that I did not follow them to the grave, in some cases.

Some have AIDS, and others have long-term diseases that will never go away, even if treated. Now I am the one who looked up to, as those who once tortured me for their own pleasure seek compassion for their wrongdoing.

Soldiers from many ranks, backgrounds, ethnicities, and diversities crossed my path throughout the years, yet some of them found it in their heart to bully me, as their way of showing their place in "the pecking order," if you will. I was never really much for "the pecking order." I only wanted to see the world and be a part of something traditionally honorable and admirable. However, as my career progressed, I found my likings to be a bit on the tender side of things. At this point in my life, relationships and failure seemed to be the only thing happening. I was not as lucky as most, unlike my little brother, who quickly commanded respect and gained the notoriety of the many ladies who graced his presents. I was quickly dismissed by the many as just another loser for the flock. I found myself beginning to lower my standards to the liking of those, though I chose not to follow in their footsteps, as later in life, their days of drugs and alcoholic ways would catch up to them. However, something inside kept me from going to that level of existence. Something held me to a higher standard of living.

Throughout my career, I would encounter the many issues of lies, deceit, deception, unfair treatment, and the unjustified promotions to others for just going along and stealing ideas and programs that I created and never received recognition for. My chest would be empty of many medals as I would be the one to stand in the ranks while many received awards for my honest doings and charity. I would be the one who would be set aside while the higher-ups took credit for my creations. I would be dismissed for being a con artist of sorts, while the fake problems of others went noticed without hesitation. I would receive nothing for the pain and suffering that

I received in combat. Where is my bronze star for the paper-pushing that I did; the long hours I put in for the good of the many? Where is my Purple Heart for the combat wounds I received? Yes, it is true I covered it up to stay in the country and not be sent home. But at any rate, the enemy wounded me, yet I never cried like the others. I doctored myself up and went on about my business, as a soldier should. I went on doing my duty, because I wanted to be noticed for the honorable thing. I even saved a sergeant from eminent death, not once but twice, and I saved nine soldiers who all slept on the ground in front of a military vehicle as the vehicle's brakes failed and began rolling toward them. I received nothing for this stupid act of saving the hateful, but they received certificates and awards for lying on the ground. I received nothing for my bravery in the line of fire as a major crime wave was foiled, yet my very own squad leader and his other soldiers received medals for not being in the area in which I was. It was I who saved the day. It was I who foiled the crime. It was I who captured eight German criminals, yet I still go unnoticed, because "they can only give out so many awards." It was I who designed a program for the army that taught thousands of soldiers, both foreign and domestic; but I received nothing for the act of designing it, implementing it, and instructing it. No, I sat on the sidelines as a superior took the credit and was promoted to command sergeant major. After a year of believing that the higher-ups knew who designed, implemented, and instructed this program, I was awestruck to find that this dishonest command sergeant major never told the higher echelons who really did the work. Again I went unnoticed, with no awards, no thank you; nothing. For over seventeen years, I lived in constant pain for saving the life of a psychotic woman after being injured in the line of duty, but I received nothing but grief for it from the many doctors who still can't seem to find anything wrong with me; those who think that something is wrong in my head. In short, I still go unnoticed even after being medically retired. I wonder why that is. I wonder why I am ever so quickly shut up by the higher ups and put out of the military. I wonder why I never received a single award for doing my damned job!

I seem to have found the answers myself. I have found in the hatred that many saw me as a threat to their pathetic existence. Many lieutenants bullied me, only because they thought they could. They told me that they would make my life a living hell for the remainder of my time in the army, when I was on my retirement leg; for what? For doing my job? Here I was, doing my job, and pretty darn good at that, and I get a handful of snot-nosed lieutenants who want to team up on the only enlisted soldier in the area. For what reason? Is it some form of initiation for not being an officer? On the other hand, is it the fact that a strong-willed, noncommissioned officer who knows a little more than they do about being in the army, over their snot-nosed college degrees, intimidates them? I guess I made them feel inferior to me or something. My last days in the army left me with a very bad taste in my mouth for the military. The hate raged inside me, as I tried to steer clear of the many higher enlisted and officer ranks. The abuse that took place in my world did not make me a better person; it only made me hate that much more. It made me something I never started out being.

So, the grueling question is "How do we fix this hatred? How do we get over the fact that there are so many self-centered people out there who live off of others' honesty and pride?" The fact of the matter is that you never really get over anything. It just seems to fade on its own, with time. The pain of my first wife's affair haunted me for years. The real fact of that is that I was never there, in body and soul. I was other places in my mind and body. I was doing the noble thing for my country while Jodie came calling. When it happened with my second wife, the pain became so intense that I attempted suicide, so many times that I stopped counted when I ran out of digits. What would that solve? The fact of the matter is, people are going to do whatever it is they want to do in life. Some are honest, and others are no-so honest. Others are just downright evil. Where do I place myself? The shocking truth is that I place myself below the lot of them. I don't know why I do this, but it just seems easier to deal with life, when you are at the bottom. This is because all that is left is up.

There are those who would protest the very essence of me saying the hateful things I have said. Well, to be perfectly honest, there is another saying that goes in hand with what I am talking about. "Do onto others as you would have them do onto you." Now this is not something to be taken so literally that I would go out and cheat myself. I am saying that I have just chosen not to be the one who lowers myself to the standards of those mentioned, and many more. I have values that I still live by. Whether they are taught or learned, I have values, which in turn, gives me the respect for myself, even if no one else will give the respect that is due to me.

Now there is the PTSD, which must be addressed here. The destruction that it has caused my family, and me, as well, is overwhelming, that professional help must be obtained to better understand why I am doing what I was doing. In my case, I found myself yelling at everyone for everything. The smallest, simplest thing, would set me off. There were times I wanted to take the head off those who crossed me. Call it being hypersensitive, if you will. Every noise that you used to hear is amplified. Every look from all the people around you is noticed. No creak in the house goes unnoticed. Many are the ones who lie, cheat, hate, are dishonest, unfaithful, and just downright inhuman. Many nights have been spent on the couch, with my wife in the bed alone, after I have been spooked or startled awake and could not go back to sleep. It felt as if someone were standing right next to me as I slept. The faint sounds of the past came to the front of my very dreams, waking me in terror. There have been times I have lunged at my wife or kids after I have been startled awake, nearly choking them to death before I wake up enough to the tears and fear in their eyes. There have been times I have lashed out in extreme anger for no reason at all. I have even gone to the extreme of hurting others and myself, and seconds later, I would not know what happened. Sounds that you once knew are gone and replaced with new ones. From time to time I have caught myself day-sleeping to avoid the nightly terrors, and visa-versa. My ability to hold a job down was nearly impossible now. I cannot be hired, due to the feelings of claustrophobia, anxiety, and extreme, chronic depression, at times unannounced to me, the soldier. The very thought of ending my own life has crossed my thoughts so many times that I cannot count the many times I have put my very own gun to my head and pulled the trigger, just to hear the click of the hammer as it falls. It was my only way of seeing reality in its true light. Several times, the gun was loaded, but never fired due to the clip not being seated right. Some say it was the work of the heavens above, but I tend to go with science and God as well.

My feelings of total worthlessness set in with each day that grew old with me. I try to do something each day, but I find myself trapped into a comfort zone within the house. I rarely go outdoors, for fear of hurting others, or worse, lapsing into a combat survival frame of thinking. The simple backfire of a vehicle has set off a chain reaction in my head and has caused total chaos within my house. There are holes punched in walls, and yelling to a decibel that the neighbors could hear down the street, and the gun being placed to my head for comfort. The only thing that stops me at that point is a migraine headache, which forces me to lay down. After the sweats subside, I will reappear to the world as a normal human being once again, until the next episode. I guess this is my way of wanting my actual "real" body pain to stop or go away, and for the fears, anxieties, depression, and terror to go away, as well.

Yes, it is real to those who are experiencing this. All of this comes with being a combat soldier. There are some who are never affected by combat, and then there are those who are. It is different in all cases, due to the fact that some see more than others, and some do more then others in their careers within the military. In my case, I have been diagnosed with several issues that I care not to get into, but warrant treatment immediately.

It is true that those who go to doctors will experience a great deal of opposition from them. You will be called a fake, a liar, a phony, and more. Mostly, this has happened because I am not one of the old farts who normally frequent the VA hospitals. I have found that you basically have to be an accepted part of that society to get any kind of good or fair treatment. This is true in my case. Others I have spoken with say the same thing I do. The doctors will tell you one thing, or hide that one thing from you, then put that you are all right in your file, only to complicate your claims later and deny true cases their due compensation and pension. Most turn away, because they are so flustered over the treatment and the politics that come with the treatment you get after you leave the service. In my case, it has been pretty damned bad, if you ask me. I have caught so many doctors in lies that I cannot trust any of them. Now, when I go see one, I try to do a self-diagnosis before I go in to see if they are lying, or if they even know what it is they are supposed to treat me for. In many cases, they have bullshitted their way through my treatment, and I have had to help them. In any case, I am still in a great deal of pain, and am getting worse; even after fifteen years of being in pain. The best one I love to hear, because it has been said so much is, "everything is normal," or "within normal limits." Sometimes I try to use humor when I go to the doctors, because I am waiting for the one time they do find something wrong. I cannot seem to put my finger on it, but when someone has been in pain for over fifteen years and minimal treatment is given over that time, and you have parts that have gone totally numb, I don't think it's normal. What I do think is that someone needs to stop looking at the damn books and "LISTEN TO THE PATIENT." We know our bodies more than you do, and a degree is not everything.

Now that I have gotten that out, my gripes take us to the family and more. Sometimes when you are deployed, your significant other gets lonely. Faith is the only thing you have at that point. The hopes and dreams that each sets for one another in relationship when we part have to be strong enough for this to happen. With the military, the soldier does not have the choice to stop the war, just because the spouse is in great need of loving. The soldier, deployed where they may, feels a great deal of loss as well. We think of them as we are in heat, cold, rain, lightning, flying bullets, impacting mortars, and we even feel the great depth of loneliness that comes with being in a foreign land, away from the ones we love. Nevertheless, with the loneliness, we also feel a great deal of pride that comes with being a soldier. Being a volunteer of something so profound and great is noble, in its own right. Being able to travel the world many times over is fabulous, in its own right; but being able to give someone freedom in an oppressed land, and seeing the gratification in their eyes is something priceless.

Being allowed the freedom to do things is something we Americans take for granted every day. We, as a spoiled nation, needed a spanking, and we got one with September 11. That was a wake-up call, to say the very least. Now it is time to change for the better and become America; the great American melting pot, as I learned it. We should not be changing for other countries and their people, if they want to live in America. They should be changing to meet our standards. For starters, learn to speak English. If I came to your country, which I probably have already, I at least tried to learn your language, so now it is your turn. If you do not like our laws, then get the hell out. No one asked you to come here.

My last days in the army left me with a very bad taste in my mouth for the military. The hate raged inside me as I tried to steer clear of higher enlisted and officer ranks. The abuse that took place in my world did not make me a better person; it only made me hate that much more. It made me something I never started out being.

At any rate, my fears of being a four-time combat veteran are to the extreme, like many others out there. You are not alone, ladies and gentlemen. We have a real disease, and that is called PTSD, or Post Traumatic Stress Disorder, and it comes from doing what you love doing. In my case, which is different from many others, I have caught myself yelling for nothing, snapping at people I don't know, and saying very hateful things that I would not likely say if I was the way I was before I joined the military. It is all a part of our upbringing and society combined. In some cases, drugs are needed to treat the disease, and other cases, counseling helps. But whatever the case, you are not alone out there. Seek help at your local VA hospitals and military installations. If that is not good for you, then seek help anywhere. Get the answers for the pains you have, and get them fast, before it destroys your life, as it has mine. As a young teenager, I grew up a confident, but reserved, child with little care for the materialistic world. Playing out in the yard was a passing of the time for me, in my world of dirt and weeds, as was riding my banana-seated bicycle with the chopper handlebars. Those were the days when cool was cool, and that was all that mattered.

I now spend my days fixing the many issues that have come and stood before me, and trying to live with that which I can no longer reverse the effects of. Speaking to you from deaths doorstep, I now take one day as it comes, and have learned the valuable lessons of being patient. I can honestly say to myself, and you all, that I never gave in.

I now long for the typical childhood fights with my younger brother, but miles separate us from one another, making us grow apart even more with time. It has literally been years since our last conversation. The feeling I get when we are on the phone is that of hate and distrust. It is as if I have something to prove to him, or that I owe something to him from our past; as if I am not good enough for his caliber of human race. This year, I took the liberty of calling for Christmas and New Years, as I do every year, but they never return my calls, nor do they ever answer their phones. There are probably the most reachable people in the world, with their cellular phones, home phones, and e-mail addresses, but the love between my younger brother and I is literally nothing. The wall is there, but he and his side of the family refuse to open the door to this side of the family. I guess it is because I made something of myself and became an honest, professional part of society and of world culture. The vast amounts of knowledge I hold is slowly being reeled back in only for the select few.

My demons with the military are not that much different. The years spent overseas in Germany seemed great to the typical eye, but when you are alone in that huge world the pain, can grace you with the presence of extreme loneliness. My downfall was that I did not play "fantasy football" or go out and drink my life away as one of the platoon members, so I was not accepted into the life of that popular and famously easygoing clique. I quickly became an outcast for the rest of the world to follow, once I reached that part my life, as we all will. The popular ones in the platoon, along with the platoon sergeant, took great offense to the fact that I appeared to be a threat to their gambling problems, and they made sure I was out of the picture, as far as they were concerned. I mostly gained full employment, while the others in the squad had their fun, playing fantasy football and cards and drinking away their time in Germany. However, it didn't take long for me to catch on to their little game, and I began drawing a deep line in the sand over their issues, so that I was suckered into believing was my problem. At the company and platoon organizational days, I was eyeballed a great deal, as the high chain of command came around to me, trying to talk with me. Moreover, as any good platoon sergeant would do, they quickly ushered me off to work on the road, or on something away from the party.

I pretty much stayed a country boy at heart, and I will always be. This life is one of being true to yourself and remaining honest, despite the odds that come your way, like seeing the masses in front of me, with their typical religious bullshit and how they say they are so honest, yet the very next day, they are the most evil sons of bitches that ever walked the earth. Of course, they will go to church on the weekends and pray their little hearts out, in the hope that the rest of the world would forgive them. Did I mention that God might as well? This is your typical hypocrite, if you ask me. I am not saying I am perfect, just honest to myself. It seems to carry more weight that way. Honesty is the best policy, and it gets you further in life then any cheating act, which has to provide to the masses of the blind.

Most called this the PTSD. For those of you who do not understand this. PTSD for soldiers is different then that of civilians. Anyone can get PTSD and still have a productive life. However, as a soldier, the choice is no longer there. As soldiers, we have to endure things that the average individual would not even think of enduring, such as extreme weather conditions, over and over again; deaths left and right; dealings with other countries' people; and the extreme stressors of traveling to foreign lands that tend to mess up your biological clock, and the endless nights of no sleep, or of loud noises and terror. After a while, the terror begins to take hold of your mind and it starts to play little tricks on you. In most cases, they are a lifetime treatment. Now, I am no doctor, but I know what is going on in my head, and I cannot seem to stop it. There are times I lash out, in anger, over nothing. There are other times I am crying over nothing, and am hearing voices in my head that are not even there, but wake me up at all hours of the night. In most cases, I cannot go back to sleep, because the slightest snap of a twig outside my house will keep me awake. If I find myself sleeping on the couch and the kids would try to wake me up, from time to time I scare my sons to death by coming up off the couch as if they were the enemy. Their eyes stare at me in fear and disbelief. After I become fully awake from my ordeal, and I see the fear in their eyes, I become ashamed of what I have done. I am afraid that I will hurt them or my wife one day, and I do not want that to happen.

I can honestly tell you and myself alike, that I never gave in. I never showed them that I could be broken, nor did I allow myself to fall prey to a lower standard of being. I always kept my courage, my honesty, my loyalty, and most of all, my honor intact, no matter how hard it became. Never give in, because once you do, then the other side has won the battle over you. In my case, I found that higher purpose of living for me: It was my time to go. My time to shine had been spent on something I never really spent it on. If you do not get it by now, then listen closely: "There comes a time in your life when you just have to say 'fuck it,' and 'stop the presses,' and just leave." There are going to be times when you feel like doing this, but that is not the time. I did not give in. I did not quit. I merely let go of the rope and fell to my death, before allowing the stubborn vultures to eat me to death. It came time for me to give back the ropes they stole and let them hang themselves.

In any case, they did just that. They lost a great person, a great noncommissioned officer, and a great leader of soldiers. You ask, how did it get to this? I became this way, because I was too valuable to the good, and I did not follow the "lower standards" that they did. I had higher standards, and I lived by the upbringing that I learned over the years. I swore that I would change a great deal as I grew up, and I did. I never allowed myself to be compromised, and that is why, I stayed true to myself. I may not have my career, but who wants a career where you have no say in anything that goes on around you; where you are a puppet and have to play games to get results; where you have to hate and learn to hate your very own? I have even learned, or have been taught to hate races, religions, factions, and people in general. I am what some would call the byproduct of hate within American society. That is not a life for me, and if you look at the numbers, there are a great deal of others who are following in my footsteps. They, too, are realizing that there is much more to life than a paycheck.

Therefore, with that said, I leave you with the thoughts of a new life and why I committed career suicide. It was my time; my time to die gracefully, without the fear of being a nobody.

ABOUT THE AUTHOR

Thomas R. Schombert is a disabled veteran and devoted husband and father, who was born in Waterloo, New York, and raised in Tucson, Arizona, and became a non-fiction writer after rekindling his passion for writing. Inspiration came from his eighth-grade teacher, back in Arizona, after Thomas wrote his very first short story called "What Happened to the World." Twenty-five years later, Thomas has produced his very first trilogy; *Diaries of a Soldier*, *Bucket Head*, and *Cannibal Boy*, based on actual occurrences in his life. Follow the novels to a place and time when Thomas was a child, to his recovery from chronic Post-Traumatic Stress Disorder. This career soldier was on his way to the top when his career was cut short after he committed career suicide and nearly had his life taken from him. He now resides in Killeen, Texas, with his wife and two sons. Experience the horrors of PTSD in the first book; relive the haunting that came out of it through his second book; then find out how he cured himself and his anger in the third book.

Printed in the United States
50423LVS00001B/127-219